CONAN
THE
BARBARIAN

He flourished in an age undreamed of, when gleaming kingdoms flung themselves across a bleak world like dark mantles beneath the brilliant stars—the Hyborian age when wizards cast spells; and supernatural beings and men ambitious for power roamed the earth. It was also his age . . . Conan, the magnificent; Conan, the barbarian king.

DINO DE LAURENTIIS
presents
An EDWARD R. PRESSMAN Production

ARNOLD SCHWARZENEGGER
JAMES EARL JONES

"CONAN THE BARBARIAN"

starring
SANDAHL BERGMAN
and
MAX VON SYDOW as King Osric

Written by JOHN MILIUS and OLIVER STONE
Music by BASIL POLEDOURIS
Associate Producer EDWARD SUMMER
Executive Producers D. CONSTANTINE CONTE
and EDWARD R. PRESSMAN
Produced by BUZZ FEITSHANS
and RAFFAELLA DE LAURENTIIS
Directed by JOHN MILIUS

A UNIVERSAL Release

CONAN THE BARBARIAN

L. Sprague De Camp and Lin Carter

Based on a Screenplay
by John Milius and Oliver Stone

BANTAM BOOKS
TORONTO · NEW YORK · LONDON · SYDNEY

CONAN THE BARBARIAN
A Bantam Book / May 1982

ISBN 0-553-22544-8

Published simultaneously in the United States and Canada

Contents

Foreword

Come with us, O readers, to a world where gleaming cities raise silver spires against the stars, sorcerers cast spells from subterranean lairs, baleful spirits stalk crumbling ruins, primeval monsters crash through jungle thickets, and the fate of kingdoms is balanced on the blades of broadswords brandished by heroes of preternatural might and valor. In this world men are mighty, women are beautiful, problems are simple, and life is adventurous, and nobody has even heard of inflation, the petroleum shortage, or atmospheric pollution!

Heroic fantasy, also called swordplay-and-sorcery fiction, traces its ancestry back to ancient epics and medieval romances. Modern heroic fantasy was invented—or, more accurately, re-invented—by William Morris in England in the 1880s. Lord Dunsany, Eric R. Eddison, and others in the United Kingdom further revitalized it, and in the United States, Robert E. Howard launched it with his stories of King Kull and Conan the Cimmerian.

Robert Ervin Howard (1906–36) was born in Peaster, Texas, and lived out his adult life in Cross Plains, a town of 1,500 at the center of the state. A shy and moody child, he became a voracious bookworm and a body-builder who enhanced his naturally powerful physique by boxing, weight-lifting, and riding. He was unconventional and hot-tempered, given to emotional extremes and violent likes and dislikes. After high school, several minor jobs, and some non-credit courses at a local college, he plunged into full-time pulp-magazine writing. By the 1930s he was making a respectable living as a prolific author of adventure, boxing, detective, fantasy, science-fiction, and Western stories.

Conan, who evolved from his earlier hero King Kull, took shape in 1932. As Howard put it, Conan "grew up in my mind . . . when I was stopping in a little border town on the lower Rio Grande. . . . He simply stalked full grown out of oblivion and set me to work recording the saga of his adventures. . . . Some mechanism in my subconsciousness took the dominant characteristics of various prize-fighters, gunmen, bootleggers, oil field bullies, gamblers, and honest workmen I have come in contact with, and combining them all, produced the amalgamation I call Conan the Cimmerian."

Conan was not Robert Howard in a bearskin breechclout; neither was Howard a Conan in khakis and a cowboy hat. Conan was an idealization of the sort of person Howard thought he would have liked to be: an irresponsible, lawless, footloose, hell-raising, predatory adventurer, devoted to wine, women, and strife. Save for his quick temper and a chivalrous attitude toward women, Howard and Conan had virtually nothing in common. Whereas Conan is portrayed as a pure extrovert, a roughneck with few inhibitions and a rudimentary conscience, Howard was sensitive, courteous, puritanical, bookish, introverted, meticulously honest, and—though he denied it—intellectual. He was the victim of such an exaggerated devotion to his mother that, when she lay dying, he put into effect a long-held plan to die with her.

The Conan stories are laid in Howard's imaginary Hyborian Age, 12,000 years ago between the sinking of Atlantis and the beginnings of recorded history. In that far-off time, Howard assumed, supernatural beings roamed the earth and magic worked. Eighteen Conan stories were published in Howard's lifetime, and he left several others, ranging from complete manuscripts to mere synopses and fragments.

These stories long moldered in the crumbling files of old pulp magazines and remained the private enthusiasm of a small circle of connoisseurs. In the 1940s and 50s, they began to reach a slightly larger audience through the publication of small hard-cover editions by specialty publishers.

In 1951 I discovered a cartonful of Howard's unpublished stories in the custody of the literary agent for his estate. Later other unpublished stories turned up. With the help of a younger colleague, Lin Carter, I edited the stories, completed the unfinished ones, and added them to the saga. Together Carter and I have written a number of additional stories, including several novels, about the invincible barbarian hero. By 1980, twenty Conan paperbacks had been published.

Conan the Barbarian is the novelization of the script of the first motion picture about the giant barbarian adventurer. It was written by myself in collaboration with Lin Carter, with additional material by Catherine Crook de-Camp.

Altogether, my wife Catherine and I have been involved with Conan for thirty years. It has been my great pleasure to have her collaborate with me on this work. We hope that readers not already aware of the Conan saga will so enjoy this work that they will seek out and read the other twenty books about the barbarian hero.

L. Sprague de Camp

Prologue

Know, O Prince, that between the years when the oceans drank Atlantis and the gleaming cities, and the rise of the sons of Aryas, there was an age undreamed of, when shining kingdoms lay spread across the world like blue mantles beneath the stars. And thither came Conan, a thief, a reaver, a slayer, to tread the jeweled thrones of the Earth beneath his sandaled feet.

And know yet further, O Prince, that in that half-forgotten age, the proudest kingdom in the world was Aquilonia, reigning supreme in the dreaming West. And this same Conan ruled from the throne of Aquilonia as Conan the Great, the mightiest lord of his day. And many were the tales spun about him as he was in his youth, wherefore it is now difficult to perceive the truth amid the many legends.

THE NEMEDIAN CHRONICLES

I

The Sword

Privileged was I, Kallias of Shamar, above all my brethren amongst the scribes of Aquilonia, to have heard from the lips of my king, Conan the Great, the story of his travails and the high adventures that befell him along the way to the summit of his greatness. Here is the tale as he told it to me in the later days of his reign, when age had laid its fell hand upon him, albeit lightly.

On a rocky ridge swept clear of snow, a man and a boy braced themselves against the fury of the storm. All about them, like a demon, the night wind howled. Lightning rent the tortured sky, smiting rocks asunder and lashing the shuddering earth with a whip of fire. The man, burly and bearded like a troll, appeared in the fitful light to be of gigantic stature as he stood, legs apart, his massive frame wrapped in furs against the bite of the wind. The boy, likewise shielded from the cold, was perhaps nine years old.

Flinging back his cloak to float like a flag against the nighted sky, the man drew from its scabbard an enormous two-handed sword, the weapon of a god. As he chanted an ancient rune spell, compounded of strange words and an unearthly rhythm, he thrust the blade upward into the heart of the tempest. With mighty legs outspread against the

3

buffetings of the wind, he brandished the splendid sword aloft, while the lowering clouds churned about him, as if the brand had pierced and wounded the very firmament.

"Harken, Conan!" shouted the man above the roar of the storm. "Fire and wind are born in the womb of the heavens, the children of the sky gods. And the mightiest of the gods is Father Crom, who ruleth earth and heaven and the broad and restless sea. Many secrets there be, whereof Crom is master; but the greatest of these is the secret of steel, a secret which the gods taught not to men but jealously guarded in their inmost hearts."

The boy stared up into the huge man's face, as stern in the inconstant light as the granite outcrop on which they stood. The man took the measure of his words, while the shrieking wind tore at his beard as if to silence him.

"Once," the deep voice began again, "giants dwelt within the earth. Mayhap they dwell there still. Crafty and wise were they, the fashioners of stone and wood, the miners of gems and gold; and in the darkness of chaos, they befooled even Crom, the Father of Gods. By their wiles they stole from him the most precious possession of the immortals: the secret of the silvery metal that, when bent, springs into shape again.

"Greatly was Crom enraged. The earth trembled, and the mountains opened. With blasts of wind and bolts of fire, Crom smote the earth giants; and they fell down; and the earth swallowed them forever. Closing its rocky lips, the earth gulped them down into the bowels of the world, the unknown place where dark things creep and crawl, the place whereof man knoweth naught."

The man's eyes blazed like blue flames amid smoldering coals; and his thick black hair, caught by a fierce gust, spread out like the wings of an eagle. Young Conan shuddered.

"The battle won," the man went on, "the gods departed for their celestial realm; but, wrathful still, they overlooked the secret of the beaten metal and left it upon the battlefield. There the first men found it, the Atlanteans of legend, our ancestors before the dawn of history."

Conan began to speak; but the man lifted a warning hand. "We, who are men, now hold the secret of steel. But we are not gods; neither are we giants. We are but mortals, weak and foolish; and our days are numbered. Be wary of steel, my son, and hold it in respect; for it carries within it a mystery and a power."

"I do not understand, Father," faltered the boy.

The man shook his black mane. "You will in time, Conan. Before a man is worthy to bear a sword of steel in battle—a weapon such as the gods once bore against the giants—he must learn its riddle. He must understand the ways of steel. Know that in all the world you can trust no one, neither man nor woman nor beast, neither spirit nor demon nor god. But you can trust a blade of well-forged steel."

The man cupped his son's small hands within his own and, curling the boy's fingers about the hilt of the great sword, said; "The heart of a man is like a piece of unworked iron. It must be hammered by adversity and forged by suffering and the challenges flung by the thoughtless gods, nigh unto the point of breaking. It must be purged and hardened in the fires of conflict. It must be purified and shaped on the anvil of despair and loss.

"Only when your heart has become as steel will you be worthy to wield a keen-edged sword in battle and win against your enemies, as did the gods when they conquered the dark giants. When you have mastered the mysteries of steel, my son, your sword will be your very soul."

All his life, Conan remembered those words, spoken by his sire on that lightning-riddled night. In time he began to comprehend the cryptic phrases, to understand the message that his father had striven to impart: out of suffering is born strength; only through pain and deprivation does a human heart become as strong as steel. But many and long were the years that passed before this wisdom became fully his.

Conan likewise remembered another night, a fortnight earlier, when the moon was an opalescent disk hung in the clear black sky like a silvern skull on a sable shroud. The snow glistened in the eerie light, and a chill wind moaned through the snow-tipped pines as he walked through the sleeping village, down the rough road that led to his father's smithy. There a fire blazed red, beating back the darkness. The firelight splashed with shifting hues of gold and crimson the smith's leathern apron and cinder-scorched trousers. It gleamed on his sweat-beaded brow and flickered across the face of the boy, who watched, open-mouthed, from the doorway.

Tirelessly, the smith drove the bellows. Then, grasping a pair of long-handled tongs, he drew forth from the heart of the furnace a dazzling length of white-hot iron, flattened and glowing. As he placed it on the anvil and began to hammer it into shape, each ringing blow sprayed a shower of sparks into the ruddy gloom of the forge.

When the cooling core of iron had turned from white to yellow to dusty red, the smith replaced it in the furnace and resumed his pushing on the bellows. At last he glanced toward the door and saw the boy. His stern gaze gentled.

"What are you doing here, son? It's time you were abed."

"You told me I could watch you turn the iron into steel, Father."

"Aye, so I did. With luck, the forging will be done tonight. The folk hereabouts think Nial the smith something of a warlock, turning iron into steel; and I would not disappoint them."

In truth, the smith was something of a godling to his neighbors; he had come out of the southlands, bearing within his breast an arcane art—the secret of steel—that precious inheritance from the ancient Atlanteans, believed lost and forgotten by all who lived in this darkling age.

As the boy approached, the smith again withdrew the iron from the furnace. "Stand back, Conan; for the sparks fly high. I would not see you harmed."

The anvil rang like a bronzen bell, giant-smitten. Fountains of sparks rose and fell before the toiling smith. Slowly the glowing length of iron assumed the shape of a mighty sword blade. Raising the metal in the tongs, he squinted along the edge, detected a curvature, and pounded it out with a few deft strokes.

After a final heating and inspection, Nial thrust the glowing brand into a vat of water, to temper the malleable metal before its final transformation into steel. The core hissed like a serpent, and a cloud of steam swirled up to invest the smith—for a moment only—in the diaphane garments of a god.

"Fetch me yonder bucket of charcoal," said Nial to his awe-struck son. "To make steel strong yet flexible, the blade must now be baked at a constant temperature, as in a charcoal bed. This is the secret possessed of the folk of Atlantis; this is the knowledge I brought hither from the south when I fled my former clan. See, thus I let the fire cool. . . ."

As the blade lay for days buried beneath a blanket of hot coals, Conan watched his father toil over the remaining tasks. The crossguard he fashioned with cunning into the form of a stag's antlers. The two-handed grip he wrapped with string made from the gut of forest tigers. The pommel itself, of steel weighted to crush the skulls of foes, he cast in the likeness of the hooves of elk.

When at last the weapon was assembled, it was a thing of bright enchantments, of memorable beauty. The polished blade flashed like a mirror, reflecting sunshine and thunder-clouds, as if the very fabric of the metal were somehow imbued with the spirits of the air.

"Is it done at last, Father?" asked the boy one evening.

"All but one thing," rumbled the smith. "Come, and you shall see."

In after years Conan remembered how rolling thunder-heads blotted out the stars as his father led him from the village of log dwellings into the upper reaches of the snow-clad mountain. As they clambered upward, the wind rose, biting the furs that sheltered them. They traversed white-lipped crevices, rough, flinty slopes, and bald out-crops where scarcely a toehold could be found. Thunder rumbled as they reached the summit. Then the storm broke.

Thus, in the fury of the elements, was the mystic rite performed to render the sword invincible.

Even upon the heels of that wild night of storm and incantation, Conan came to learn his first lesson in suffer-ing. Cruel that lesson was and far too early for so young a child. But the northlands are bleak; life therein is harsh; and the hand of every stranger is lifted in enmity against his fellows.

Night shambled off before the silent footfalls of a frozen dawn. The waning moon, disconsolate, draped her face in a drifting veil of clouds. Only a tired wind stirred the silence as it whispered through the branches of the leafless trees.

Suddenly, the quiet was fractured by the clamor of horsemen who crashed through the bushes. Their horses, shod in iron, shattered the thin ice of the stream that paralleled the village. Dark and grim, wearing leather armor scaled with iron, and holding axes, spears, and swords in their gloved hands, the raiders swept down upon the hamlet.

Men and women, startled from their slumbers, awoke to find the rutted road between their huts blocked by mounted strangers. Confused and disorganized, the villagers emerged from their homes, clutching their coarse woollens about them and shouting at the invaders. One woman shrieked as she snatched a toddler from beneath a horse's prancing hooves. With a roar of triumph, the rider leaned from his saddle to thrust his lance between the shoulders of the fleeing mother. She staggered as the spearhead burst into view between her breasts; then, limp as a rag doll, she was borne along, until the soldier, with an oath, tore the shaft loose from her mangled flesh.

"The Vanir!" roared Nial the smith as, swinging his blacksmith's hammer, he plunged from the mouth of his hut.

Standing on his doorstep, the boy Conan stared in bewilderment, searching for order in the chaos all about him. But there was no order. A young girl darted past him, white with terror. Behind her sped a lean black hound, its jaws agape, its red tongue flapping. An instant later, the beast had pulled her down and worried her throat to crimson ribbons. Before Conan's unbelieving eyes, one of her hands flopped like a beached fish on the mud-spattered snow.

A naked Cimmerian hunter, armed with a huge axe, sprang howling into the turmoil and swung his weapon like a wheel of death. It caught one raider on the thigh, hewing his leg away. Shrieking, the Van fell from his saddle, his blood spurting a scarlet arc across the snow. Above the clatter of hooves, the clank of iron, and the war cries of the Vanir, Conan heard the shrill wails of women and the screams of the maimed and dying.

Conan's father pushed past his son, vanished into his hut, and reappeared with the great sword. The ensorcelled blade, which glittered like frozen lightning against the morning sky, swept all before it. Van after Van fell from his mount with entrails spilling out across the trampled, muddy snow.

Shaking off the paralysis of fear, Conan snatched up a fallen knife and dove into the fray, determined to stand beside his sire. Although the press of struggling men was too thick for the boy to hack through, his blade hamstrung one towering dark warrior, who stumbled into the path of the blacksmith's sweeping sword. The invader's head, sheared cleanly off, spun through the air like a well-tossed ball, to plop into the mud at Conan's feet. The boy leaped back, nape-hairs astir, eyes almost starting from their sockets.

Now other Cimmerians ran to make a stand with Nial the smith. But the invaders were mounted and well armed, with breasts sheathed in bronze and iron, while the villagers were half-naked, and bore only the simple implements they had been able to snatch up. Some carried hoes and rakes; others had retrieved their weapons. A few were armed with shields of boiled hides stretched on wooden frames; but these afforded indifferent protection against the pounding weight of Vanir iron.

Unable to reach his father, Conan sought out his mother; but in the turmoil and cacophony of the battle, he could not find her. He ran and ducked and dodged as men and horses thundered past. On every side he beheld scenes of mayhem and slaughter. A freshly severed arm lay in the snow, trickling blood; while its fingers still gripped the shaft of a spear. A woman, bearing her babe to safety, hurried by. She stumbled and fell in the slippery mud. A heartbeat later, a hoof crushed her skull, and her puling infant fell into a bank of blood-stained snow.

An old man was arrested in mid-cry, as a bronze-tipped arrow transfixed his tongue. Another crouched in a

pool of icy mud, pawing at his face. Conan realized dimly
that one eyeball hung by a strand of tissue and that the man,
crazed by pain, was trying to restore the eye to its proper
resting place.

Over the crash and clamor, Conan heard his father's
uplifted voice: "The horses! Kill the horses!" So saying, the
smith brought down a war horse, which screamed like a
stallion beneath the gelding iron as his sword sheared
through its spine.

Conan at last spied the lithe figure of his mother,
standing barefoot in the snow. There was a majesty about
her as she faced the enemy, her face flushed with fury, her
hair cascading over her shoulders, and her hands clenched
about the handle of a broadsword. Heaped before her lay
the bloody remains of several Vanir and their merciless
dogs. As the boy hurtled toward her, she glanced at her
son's tousled mane of coarse black hair, so like his father's,
and grasped her weapon with renewed determination.

Looking up, Conan glimpsed a gigantic figure bestrid-
ing a sable stallion, like a statue, dark and motionless.
Horse and rider loomed above the brow of a hillock at the
edge of the village and stared down upon the scene of
carnage. The child could not discern the features of the
giant form, but his frantic eye was arrested by the emblem
that the horseman bore upon his armored breast and
iron-bound shield.

It was a strange device: two black serpents face to face,
their tails so interwoven that they might be one, and
between them, supported by their coils, the disk of a black
sun. The symbol, unfamiliar as it was, filled Conan's heart
with fear and foreboding.

Not far away, most of the men and youths who had
survived the charge and its resultant slaughter had formed a
living shield about their smith. Towering above even the
tallest of the other Cimmerians, Nial cried out his martial
encouragements, as metal belled against metal and masked
the screams of the dying. The Vanir fell back; when their
horses, wild-eyed, wheeled and danced before the rude
weapons of the defenders.

As caution stayed the raiders, from the swelling

ground, the mailed figure raised one gloved hand in a gesture of command. Dawnfire flashed from his iron helmet, which, concealing his features, lent him an aura of terrible power.

"They'll bring up their archers," whispered Conan's mother. "They'll cut our menfolk down as they stand beyond the range of our Cimmerian steel."

"Crom help us!" murmured the boy.

Conan's mother gave him an icy glance. "Crom does not heed the prayers of men. He scarcely hears them. Crom is a god of frosts and stars and storms, not of humankind."

Soon were the words of Maeve, the blacksmith's wife, proven true. A hail of arrows whistled through the dawn, to thud against the wooden huts, to glance from shields, and to sink, feather-deep, into naked flesh. Again and again the deathly rain of Vanir arrows swept the cluster of defenders, until the shield-wall sagged and crumbled.

At last the gigantic figure upon the hillock spoke, his deep, unearthly voice tolling like an iron bell. "Loose the hounds!"

Snarling and snapping, the red-tongued dogs panted down the slope, their flying forms silhouetted against the vermilion dawn. One Cimmerian fell, gurgling, with a hound at his throat. Another speared one beast in mid-leap. A third yelled hoarsely as wolf-sharp fangs closed on the muscles of his upper arm. And the wall of shields came apart, as men turned to strike with notched and blunted swords at the vicious animals.

"Archers!" boomed the dark giant. "Let fly another round!"

A hissing hail of death fell on the surviving few. Bodies writhed in the trampled snow, as their fellow villagers staggered back, their hide shields pierced by the flying shafts. For a moment Conan saw his father standing alone, his shield bristling with arrows. Then a shaft caught the blacksmith in the leg, piercing the muscle of his upper thigh. The injured limb gave way beneath him. With a choked curse, he fell and lay on his back in the frozen slush.

One hand crawled across the ice, inching toward the hilt of the great steel sword. An arrow pinned his hand to the ground. Then the dogs were at him.

It was soon over.

II

The Wheel

Now horsemen crested the rise and thundered down among the huts, their merciless swords cutting down all who resisted. Lighted torches wheeled through the icy air to thud upon the rush roofs of the defenseless houses and set them ablaze. Thus were flushed out into the open all who had taken refuge within their homes.

Whooping riders pounded along the rutted lane, spearing the young, the old, and the wounded. Maeve impaled one leering fellow who bent from his galloping horse to seize her. She smiled thinly as his torn body toppled from the saddle to lie sprawling in the mud. A sweep of the Cimmerian woman's sword hamstrung another animal. As the beast fell kicking, Conan sprang upon the rider, writhing in agony beneath his steed, and sliced open his throat.

But the defenders were outnumbered. Their ranks thinned rapidly. Abruptly, their resistance ended. Dazed and dejected, all the survivors threw their weapons at the booted feet of their conquerors—all, that is, but Maeve, wife of Nial and mother of Conan. Eyes ablaze in a face drained of color, she leaned on the pommel of her broadsword, stunned and struggling for breath, while her son stood beside her, his small knife held at the ready.

13

At last the mounted giant on the knoll moved. As spurs struck its glossy black flanks, the quivering stallion sprang into motion. With a measured control more terrible to witness than the careless speed of fury, the commander of the marauders picked his way down the slope and along the ruts of trampled snow stained with the blood of the dead or dying. Although his features were masked by his horned iron helm, to those who watched, he stood against the morning sky, a veritable demon-king borne on a steed that seemed no earthly horse at all but a creature from the very depths of Hell.

When the grim apparition passed them, the Vanir raiders bowed and gave voice to an orchestrated chant: "Hail to Commander Rexor! Hail to Rexor! And to Doom . . . Doom . . . Thulsa Doom. . . ."

Their leader turned off the road and, for a moment, vanished from sight behind the soot-blackened wall of a burned-out hut. As if a cloud had lifted, the Vanir brightened and drifted nearer to the lone woman who, with her man-child, stood defiant still.

Jeering with coarse ribaldry and obscene suggestions, two of the raiders reached playful spears toward the breast of the half-naked woman. Maeve batted aside one weapon with the flat of her sword, and the Van dodged backwards, laughing. But his comrade was less fortunate. Swinging her long blade above her head, Maeve caught her tormentor across the back of his hand and inflicted a deep cut. As the man leaped aside, his spear fell from a hand that hung as limp as a dead thing. Cursing and baring his teeth in a snarl, he reached for his sword with his uninjured hand.

Just then the fur-cloaked figure of the commander, grim as death, emerged from the shadow of the hut. Not a word was spoken, but the wounded man wilted and withdrew. In response to a signal, another soldier sprang forward to grasp the bridle of the warhorse, while his master swung to the ground. With an imperious gesture, Rexor pointed back along the rutted roadway on which lay the smith, his inert hand a finger's length away from the weapon that was his final masterpiece.

Eager to do the huge man's bidding, another foot soldier sped between the two rows of smoldering huts, to the place where Nial the smith had made his stand. Lifting the blade, which no man could have wrested from Nial's living grasp, he hastened to bring it to his leader. Maeve watched the man's approach through slitted ice-blue eyes. Conan stared in fearful fascination; for it was borne in upon him with hideous certainty that his father lived no more.

When Rexor received the weapon, he raised it to study its splendid craftsmanship in the sun's slanting rays. As the metal, uplifted, shimmered in the brighter light, Conan in vain fought back the sobs that choked him. His mother touched his shoulder. A soldier laughed.

A shudder suddenly erased the grins from the faces of those still ringed around the embattled pair. Conan looked up, as high against the rising sun a standard, set upon an ebon pole, came slowly into view. Suspended from a wooden frame adorned with the horns of beasts, the rich fabric of the standard hung immobile in the still air. Embroidered on the cloth, the boy saw once more the symbol that long would haunt his dreams—the ominous, emblazoned symbol of writhing serpents upholding the orb of a sable sun.

A grisly fringe of scalps dangled from the frame, and gaunt skulls grinned mockingly from the spikes that adorned the upper reaches of the structure. Even Rexor bowed his head as that hideous standard entrapped the eastern light and was incarnadined thereby. Conan recoiled when he saw the bearer of the banner, a deformed thing, more beast than man, despite his iron helm and armored leathern garments. The pride with which he raised aloft his fear-inspiring device declared his lack of all humanity.

Behind this misshapen offspring of the devil rode a magnificent figure, resplendent in armor of overlapping leaves, gleaming like the scales of a serpent in the opalescent light. A bejeweled helmet clung to his head and covered his nose and cheekbones, so that only his eyes, flaming with unholy fires, were visible.

The steed he rode was very like its master: lean, graceful, and aglitter with jeweled trappings. Its eyes, too, burned with the light of living coals. On such a steed, thought Conan, might devils from the nether parts of Hell come howling up to ravage the green hills of earth.

As the great beast paced the bloodstained snow, under the gloved guidance of its rider, all the Vanir bowed low, repeating one word like an incantation: "Doom . . . Doom . . . Doom!"

The giant Rexor leaped forward to hold the hell-steed's bridle as his master dismounted. The two exchanged but a word or two, then turned to scrutinize the Cimmerian woman, who stood, tense and level-eyed, grasping her broadsword. As Maeve returned their gaze and sensed the menace in it, like a mother panther prepared to defend her cub, she raised her weapon and moved one foot into position for a strike.

The man in the jeweled helmet, still studying her with cool appraisal, drew off his glove and reached out one lean hand to accept from his lieutenant the sword of Nial the smith. Rexor bowed as he handed the weapon to his master.

"Doom . . . Doom . . . Doom!" intoned the Vanir once again; and as he listened, Conan perceived that this was no mere word of welcome that the raiders chanted. It was a portentous name—a name to conjure with, a name to fear.

Doom, a lithe figure in his serpentine mail, sauntered up to the embattled Cimmerians, mother and son. As he approached, his slitted eyes studied the sheer perfection of the weapon in his hands. Focusing his entire attention on the fine blade, or so it seemed, he turned it this way and that, admiring its razor edge, its flawless balance, its exquisite workmanship. Mirror-bright, the steel flashed in the low sun's rays and immersed the waiting boy in a scintillating river of light.

As the ring of armed men parted, Maeve drew up her splendid body, raised her broadsword, and set her jaw. A swift intake of breath between parted lips served as a warning of her intention.

Suddenly Doom appeared to notice her. He doffed his jeweled helm, revealing a lean-jawed, darkly handsome face. A small smile flickered across his thin lips, and something akin to admiration flashed red in his coal-black eyes. The woman stood as if transfixed, fascinated yet repelled by his commanding presence and the overpowering aura of male sexuality that radiated from his person.

"Doom . . . Doom . . . Doom!" shouted the motionless Vanir warriors in unison.

For a long moment, Doom stared into the wide eyes of Conan's mother. Her finely-sculpted breasts, kissed by the roseate light, rose and fell with rapid breathing. Then, careless of the woman's upraised sword, he strolled past her, moving well within the range of her steel, but ignoring it, as if peril did not exist for such as he. The grace and bearing of his supple body, as he walked past the Cimmerian woman, was sensual, inviting, and vibrant with virility; but Maeve neither moved nor spoke. She remained utterly immobile, seemingly enthralled, as a partridge is fabled to be by the enticements of a serpent's gaze.

Once past her, with a gesture so casual as to look effortless, Doom swept the great sword upward with incredible skill and strength. The ugly sound the blade made as it struck rang loudly in the chill silence.

Without a cry, or even a gasp, Maeve fell, as a tree falls before the axe of the forester. Dazed with horror, the boy Conan stared in disbelief as his mother's severed head rolled in the mire at his feet. Her pale face displayed neither fear nor shock nor pain, only a dreamy-eyed look of fascination.

Then as the boy, hate-filled, whipped about and aimed his knife at the broad back of Doom, the Vanir were upon him, dragging him into a snowdrift, and wresting his knife from his grasp.

As the day faded, a weary column of captives, chained one to another, trudged across an endless expanse of pristine snow, shadowed by pines. The bedraggled line, a sad remnant of what had been a close-knit Cimmerian clan, were the sole survivors of the dawn raid on their village. Old men, women, and children, the ill-clad and the injured, slipped and slid their way over the ice-coated snows and rocky outcrops into slavery.

Far behind the captives, smoke still stained the sky. Having plundered the village, seizing weapons and food and furs and hides, the Vanir had put all buildings to the torch. Even the hot coals and ashes had been trampled under the horses' hooves to scatter them, so that when spring thawed the earth, and new grass sprang up, there would exist no evidence that here had ever been a dwelling place of men.

The boy Conan staggered along, bent beneath the weight of his chain and chilled by the upland winds and the iron collar that clutched at his throat. He moved slowly, his mind a turmoil of half-memories and uncomprehending dread. He had witnessed too much bloodshed for his youthful reason to absorb. Despite his pounding heart, he felt nothing, his emotions numbed by the living nightmare of the day's events.

That endless journey into Vanaheim would ever after remain a dreamlike horror in Conan's memory, a blurred montage of startling images: fur-clad riders whirling past the bowed, staggering line of captives, scattering snow . . . the grisly standard uplifted against the sky, flaunting its emblem of tangled serpents and a black sun . . . an old man, unable to walk further, unchained from the line and speared with uncaring savagery . . . small red footprints left on the ice by the torn feet of barefoot children . . . the cold winds in the mountain passes . . . weariness and despair.

Conan never noticed when the giant Rexor and his mysterious master, Doom, parted company with the Vanir raiders. But there came a time when he realized that the two were no longer with the party; for suddenly the air seemed fresher and the sunlight brighter. Vaguely the boy wondered why those two dark, towering men, who so obviously were not men of Vánaheim, had led the attack on his village. When he dared to whisper the question to another captive, the man murmured, "I know not, boy. The Vanir doubtless paid well for the dark men's services, but I did not see the money pass."

The captives and their captors journeyed northward, winding a tortuous path through the broken hills of northern Cimmeria. Gaunt crags of naked rock thrust through their mantles of wind-piled snow, and the saw-toothed range of the Eiglophians loomed before them like a row of white-robed giants against the sapphire skies. In the pass, a late snow flurry swirled around the ill-clad slaves, stinging their eyes with bitter kisses. Then the feet of the children, chilled to insensibility, no longer felt the bite of rocks against half-frozen flesh.

Snow persisted as the Cimmerians crossed the mountains into Vanaheim, the realm of their enemies. The horsemen and their hounds were forced to range far afield to hunt game. Streams, fed by the melting snow in sheltered places, cut deep runnels in the lingering snowdrifts and supplied crystal-cold water to the captives' camping sites. Thus they survived.

At last they began to descend the far side of the mountain range. Stunted trees clung precariously to the rough land, their twisted forms looking to the boy like crooked gnomes crouching beside their tunnels. Stretches of tundra bore raw wounds where herds of reindeer had pawed the snow aside to nibble on dead grasses. Long lines of marsh fowl, northward bound, flapped by; and the honking of their mournful cries echoed the despairing bitterness in Conan's heart.

As the slaves straggled across the marshes, the boy noticed the heads of drowned tussocks emerging from water scummed with patches of floating ice; and on these tussocks he saw the first timid flowers of spring.

The journey seemed as endless as forever. But it ended at last.

One dusk, as the setting sun shot blood-red darts into the mist-veiled bosom of the land, Conan and the other captives were herded through the palisaded gateway of a Vanir town—a sizable community, which they later came to know as Thrudvang.

The footsore thralls were driven like cattle through a clutter of stone houses, half-buried in turf and roofed with thatch. At length they reached a walled enclosure within which stood several sheds. Into one of these slave pens, which offered scant protection from the elements, the newcomers were hustled to spend the lonely night sleeping on hard clay sparsely strewn with dirty straw.

At dawn, after receiving a small ration of bread and thin soup, the stronger and healthier among them were chained by rusty manacles to a massive wheel whose spokes were stout logs, polished smooth by the pressure of human hands. This wheel turned one enormous millstone upon another, grinding grain to powder beneath its ponderous weight. To this Wheel of Pain, as the slaves came to call it, Conan was chained beside other ragged, dull-eyed youths and men from lands unknown or rarely mentioned in Cimmeria. As for the captive women and girl-children of his village, they were led away to face a different, perhaps even uglier fate. Conan never heard of them again.

The Master of the Wheel was a burly man, swarthy and heavy-featured, who seemed to the laboring children to be an ogre. Day after day, as they pushed the groaning wheel in an eternal circle, he stood on the incline above the shallow pit wherein the wheel was fixed, wrapped in his greasy furs. As grim and unspeaking as an idol of stone, he stood, with only his sharp, fierce eyes moving in his leather-framed face as he watched, hawklike, to detect the laggard or the indolent.

Only when an exhausted boy fell to his knees, unable to work any longer, did he spring into action. Then a vicious rawhide whip sang its sibilant song, laying crimson welts on pitiful shoulders, until under its bite the whimpering wretch would stagger to his feet to toil once more.

So Conan and his fellows labored day after day, month after month, until time lost all meaning for them. Faces slack, eyes dull, hearts emptied of emotion, time for them contracted to the present moment only. Yesterday was mercifully obliterated from their consciousness; tomorrow was a nightmare yet undreamed. When a wheel-slave fell and could rise to toil no more, the Master summoned the ever-present Vanir guards with a curt gesture to unshackle the gasping body and bear it off—no one knew where.

Conan dully wondered at times if that was how the Vanir fed their dogs.

The seasons changed; months stumbled into years. Wheel-slaves died, only to be replaced by other slaves, reaved by the Vanir raiders. Some of the new captives were youths and men of Cimmerian stock; others were golden-haired boys from Asgard: a few were gaunt Hyperboreans with limp, flaxen locks and, it was said, a knowledge of sorcery. Not that it seemed to do them any good.

For all, life became a dreary endurance of days of grinding toil and nights of deathlike slumber. Hope died like a candle in the wind. Despair dulled Conan's senses until they became indifferent to discomfort. True, he and his fellows did receive some care, lest they become useless as draft animals. They had good food, a small fire in their quarters during winter storms, and a supply of cast-off clothing too ragged to be worth the mending. But that was all.

Ever there was the groaning Wheel of Pain, ever the pitiless blue sky above, ever the frozen slush of winter or the cracked, dry mud of summer beneath their feet. And ever the clank of the chain that bound them to the wheel.

Once and once only Conan wept, and it was but a single tear that trickled down his dirty cheek to freeze like a gem stone in the frigid wind. For a moment the boy slumped against the wheel-spoke, slick from the pressure of his sweaty palms, and prayed for an end to the unending torture, even if the end was death. But the moment passed. He shook his unshorn black mane and dashed the tear away.

There is in every heart a threshold, a point beyond which hopelessness and resignation cannot penetrate: a moment in which life and death are equal forces. At this moment, a new kind of courage is born within the heart of even the dreariest slave. The emotion that took possession of Conan's heart as he brushed away that tear was *rage* —hot and unforgiving rage.

His lips drew back from his strong teeth in a savage snarl. Wordlessly, the young Cimmerian made a vow to his indifferent northern gods: Never again, he promised, shall gods or men or devils wring from my eyes a single tear.

And he made another vow in the silence of his heart: Men shall die for this!

Then with all his strength, he leaned against the spoke of the Wheel of Pain. The wheel groaned and creaked as it began again its endless circuit.

Nurtured by the fires of rage, a new-found pride, and the courage to endure, Conan grew into a man. The years of back-breaking labor that toughened his sinews and made his muscles bulge gave his body the strength and flexibility which soft iron gains when it is heated in the furnace and pounded by the hammer of the smith. And though his days were blurred by a monotony of crushing toil, and his body held in chains, Conan found that his mind was free—free to soar like the marsh fowl on wings of hope.

Whenever the harvest proved lean, disputes arose among the Vanir. Some wished to reduce the slaves' rations; others argued that, if the slaves starved, they could not work the mill wheel, and the whole town would lack for bread. These debates often took place among the townfolk who brought their corn to be ground; and no one thought to spare the wretched slaves the furious arguments, since they were deemed too dull or ignorant to understand the spoken word.

But, having an aptitude for languages, Conan knew what was being said. He had learned to speak fluent, if accented, Vannish and had picked up a smattering of Aquilonian and Nemedian from his fellow captives. Otherwise his mind slept, save when it gnawed like a hungry wolf on the thought of revenge. He might have learned more had he drawn out his shed-mates; but he was a taciturn youth, who asked for no companionship and offered none.

"It was an error on my part," King Conan told me in *the fullness of his years. "They might have taught me to write their tongues, had I encouraged them. I did not dream that some day I should need that skill; for we knew naught of letters in Cimmeria. Knowledge should be grasped where'er it lies, for it is a jewel beyond price, as now I know."*

During one famine, a plague descended on Thrudvang. Many died; and all the drumming and chanting of the shaman did nothing to stay the disaster. The pestilence spread to the mill. Underfed and overworked, the slaves proved an easy prey. One by one, they took to coughing, suffered bloody fluxes, and succumbed.

At last the day came when Conan stood alone at the Wheel of Pain. When the Master descended to the walkway to drag out the final corpse, he said in tones of honest perplexity, "I do not know what to do with you, Cimmerian. We must have flour ere we starve; but one man cannot turn the mill alone."

"Hah!" grunted Conan. "Think you so? Place me at the outer end of the boom, and I'll show you that I can."

"Well, you shall have your chance. May your Cimmerian gods be with you!"

With his manacle relocked at the outmost position on the pole, Conan took a deep breath, strained every muscle, and pushed. The mill revolved.

For many days before new slaves were found, the young giant turned the wheel alone. Vanir from surrounding villages, bringing their meager supplies of grain to be milled, marveled at the sight. They took the measure of his magnificent shoulders and the powerful muscles in his arms and thighs. And the word spread. . . .

One day there came a break in the endless drudgery —and a visitor. Laboring at the wheel, Conan glimpsed the Master in earnest conversation with a mounted stranger, whose five attendants, with due decorum, sat their shaggy ponies at the far side of the mill enclosure. While the Master of the Wheel was dark-complected, the newcomer represented a different breed of humanity, one the young Cimmerian had never seen before.

The horseman appeared squat and bowlegged, as from a lifetime spent with legs clamped about the barrel of his steed. His fine cloak was made of unfamiliar furs, the skins of beasts unknown to the Cimmerian; and his peculiar armor was composed of plates of lacquered, overlapping leather. His eyes were narrow and slitted, his cheekbones wide, and he wore his thick red hair and ruddy beard trimmed in a fashion that seemed foreign. A pin of blue and topaz stones winked from his velvet cap, and a heavy gold chain encircled his neck.

Through eyes as black as chips of obsidian, the red-haired horseman studied the Cimmerian youth with the cool appraisal of a horse trader. As Conan, still pushing the wheel, watched indifferently, the man nodded in apparent satisfaction, dug one gloved hand into his girdle, and withdrew several small, flat squares of gold. These he handed to the Master of the Wheel, then kneed his mount forward to the edge of the mill works. The Master hurried down the ramp to stop the mill. Conan stood, docile and unresisting, as his manacle was unlocked, and a heavy wooden collar was fitted around his neck. He waited patiently, flexing his hard and callused fingers, while the Master locked the collar and handed the end of the chain to the mounted man.

The foreigner licked his lips with a pointed tongue. Then, speaking Vannish in hard gutturals, he said, "I am Toghrul. I own you now. You come."

For emphasis, he tugged on the chain as one tugs on a dog's leash. Conan stumbled forward. Recovering his balance, he looked up to find the man grinning down at him. Resentment flared in the Cimmerian's sullen eyes; a growl rumbled deep in his chest. With a burst of rage, he snatched a link and jerked it back, tearing the chain from Toghrul's grasp.

For a moment, Conan stood free, legs apart, shoulders arched, eyes blazing, as the hot breath of freedom awoke wild memories in his barbaric heart. Surprise immobilized the others. Then sharp steel rasped against leather as the Wheel-master and Toghrul's men-at-arms rushed to encircle the recalcitrant slave.

Conan's eyes glowed a volcanic blue as he glared at the ring of naked blades. Then he glanced at the Wheel of Pain, at the pole polished from its long contact with his sweaty palms, at the empty manacle that had bound his wrist in servitude. Whatever might lie ahead in the womb of time, at least he was free of the Wheel.

The fires of wrath faded from his eyes. He took a deep breath. Then, silently, he picked up the chain and handed the end to his new master. The horseman grinned.

"The animal has spirit!" he grunted. "He will make a rare spectacle in the Pit."

III

The Pit

Followed by his bodyguard on their shaggy ponies,
Toghrul trotted smartly from the town. The chain, now
wound around the pommel of his saddle, clanked against
the clumsy wooden collar that confined the neck of the
Cimmerian slave. The muscles of Conan's legs were strong
from years of toil at the wheel, and massive was his chest;
yet his thews ached, and each indrawn breath became a
strangled sob as his master quickened his pace from a trot to
an easy canter.

Stones thrust jagged edges against Conan's naked feet.
Once, when he stumbled, he was dragged along until the
pony, unsettled by the unaccustomed weight of an inert
body, slowed to a walk. Then the youth regained his footing
and forced his bruised and bleeding limbs to carry him
forward.

At length the group dismounted for their midday meal.
A skin of sour red wine and slabs of bread and cheese were
passed around. Conan, listening to the men's rude banter
while he munched his food, learned that his new owner was
a Pitmaster from Hyrkania, a land far to the east, beyond
barren Hyperborea. Around Asgard and Vanaheim, sometimes together called Nordheim or Northlands, the red-
bearded man traveled with his troupe, staging fights for the

25

amusement of local chieftains and their gaming cronies. Sometimes he lured, with promises of gold, neighborhood champions to do combat with his Pit fighters—slaves all, whose final adversary was always Death.

As dusk turned the northern sky to steel and smudged the greenery along the narrow track, the sturdy ponies and the footsore young Cimmerian reached Toghrul's encampment. Here, encircled by a rough log palisade, were several houses and sheds, a corral for the horses, and pens for the Pit slaves—men who had been selected as much for their savage truculence as for their powerful bodies and superior fighting skills.

Toghrul halted before one of the slave pens and shouted a question to the armored guards who lounged around the enclosure. Although Conan failed to comprehend all the Hyrkanian words, he gathered that his master was seeking someone named Uldin. Uldin proved to be a stocky, long-armed man with a shaven scalp, who, after exchanging words with Toghrul, the exact meaning of which the Cimmerian did not understand, unwound the chain from Toghrul's pommel and grasped it firmly in large and sinewy hands.

Speaking Vannish with a foreign accent, he muttered, "Come along, you!"

As he was led into an airless, stench-filled room, something akin to panic seized the young barbarian. He felt the presence of others, but their forms were only shadows in the darkness. Then Uldin lit the stub of a taper. In the flickering light of this pale candle, Conan saw his fellow slaves, ragged and unwashed, lying on the raw dirt floor. Silent, unmoving, they watched him, their firelit eyes reflecting scant humanity.

Uldin unlocked Conan's bulky collar and removed it. Then he faced the travel-worn youth. "What is your name?" he barked.

"Conan."

"Whence come you?"

"I am a Cimmerian. Why am I here?"

"To learn to fight," said Uldin. "What do you know of fighting?"

"Nothing," growled Conan. "I was captured eight

summers past, and I've been pushing that cursed mill wheel ever since. Before that, sometime, I fought with other boys."

"Then we'll start with barehand fighting. Take off your shirt."

The Cimmerian obeyed, peeling off his coarse tunic carefully, lest the rotten fabric tear beyond utility. The trainer studied Conan's body critically, raising the taper to complete his task.

"The wheel gave you good shoulders," he grunted. "Try to throw me."

Crouching, Conan moved toward the Hyrkanian trainer, his arms reaching out for a hold. He never understood what happened next. The short man slipped out of Conan's grasp as if he had been a column of smoke. A moment later, a foot caught the Cimmerian's ankle and sent him sprawling.

"Again!" commanded Uldin, as the befuddled youth struggled to his feet.

Conan advanced cautiously, thinking: I'll seize his neck and throw him across my hip, as we used to do as boys. But the trainer, instead of avoiding Conan's clutching arms, allowed the Cimmerian to catch his head in the crook of an elbow. Then, lithe as a panther, Uldin threw himself backwards, pulling Conan forward above him. As Uldin fell supine, he doubled up his legs, planting his feet against Conan's belly, and shoved violently upward. The youth flew over the trainer's head, to land heavily on his back. Uldin rolled to his feet and stood looking down at him with a crooked grin.

Conan rose, snarling like a wolf at bay. "Crom damn you!" he spat, and rushed upon Uldin again—only to go sprawling once more.

This time, when Conan got up, he found Uldin grinning at him like a bald-headed ape. "Go on, hate me!" rasped the Hyrkanian. "Hate will make you a better fighter. But you have much to learn. Tomorrow we'll get on with the first lesson."

Throughout that summer, Conan learned to fight for his life. In the Pit, it was fight or die. Conan fought and lived.

Conan did not become intimate with his fellow Pit
fighters. As one of them confided early in his training, it
was senseless to make friends with a man you might have to
kill lest you be killed by him.

The first time Conan was dropped into the Pit, he gave
a swift, all-encompassing glance around the place of death
or triumph. With others of Toghrul's troupe, he had been
taken in chains to Skaun, a town of the Vanir. Here the
fighters were herded into a high-roofed, barnlike structure,
wherein fires smoldered in beds of charcoal to lessen the
biting chill of early autumn.

The Pit was ten paces long, five wide, and as deep as
the height of a man. The edges were hung with crudely-
figured shields and standards of hide, painted in cranberry
red, cerulean blue, and raw earth tones.

Looking up from the enclosure, Conan saw a ring of
Vanir chieftains, sitting on crude benches and guzzling ale
from cups of horn. When they tired of handling these
vessels, they thrust the horn points into the soft earth at their
feet. Torches set in brackets encircled the upper reaches of
the Pit. The fitful light gleamed on the red manes and ruddy
faces of the men and glinted on their bracelets and pectorals
of gold and silver, embellished with uncut gemstones.
Smoke hung heavy in the air, commingling with the reek of
ill-tanned hides and baggy woollens, stiff with dirt and
rancid sweat.

The chieftains laughed, hooted, drank heavily, and
bawled obscene jests. But they eyed the fighters shrewdly
before placing bets and displayed bars of gold, precious
jewels, and fine weapons as earnest of their wagers.

Half a dozen fighters stood against the far wall of the
Pit, a group of powerful men, naked save for dirty clouts.
Their deep chests, broad backs, and muscled limbs were
smeared with grease, to afford scant hold to their opponents.
Conan recognized none of these men. Since he had heard
some muttered talk among Toghrul's people of a rival
Pitmaster, an Asa from Asgard named Ivar, the Cimmerian
inferred that the strange fighters might be of Ivar's troupe.

A second glance upward at the swilling, shouting
Vanir showed Toghrul standing to one side, talking with a

fellow whose tawny beard was streaked with gray. Conan could not hear their words as they gestured and pointed to the line of slaves in the Pit. But presently Uldin and two other men clambered down a ladder and hustled out all save the fighter who had been chosen for Conan's adversary. Those dismissed ascended the ladder and disappeared, leaving the barbarian alone with the remaining man, a gigantic Negro.

Conan stared; he had never before seen skin of ebon hue. A thousand leagues or more to the south, in the land of Kush, his father had told him, such men were said to live. The Negro's bullet head was shaven smooth. Deep in the shining mask of his heavy-featured face, the man's eyes burned with feral fires. His jaws moved rhythmically as he chewed on a handful of leaves; and as the potent narcotic entered his blood stream and ascended to his brain, the look in his eyes became inhuman, the eyes of a beast of prey.

Pretending to be feckless and bewildered, the young barbarian studied his opponent. The black was a magnificent specimen of savage manhood, his oiled body gleaming in the firelight like a statue carved from obsidian. Terrific strength slept in those massive shoulders and arms; while beneath the skin of torso and legs, muscles like writhing pythons tensed and relaxed.

When the drug had taken full charge of the Negro's brain, he sprang upon Conan like a charging tiger. In an instant his huge hands closed about the novice's throat and clamped tight, sinking into the flesh and stifling the warning growl that rose from Conan's chest. The Cimmerian's hands locked on the wrists of the black, and the two struggled together in a dance of death, swaying back and forth in an embrace as intimate as that of lovers. The Vanir chieftains howled with excitement.

Conan fought desperately for breath, tensing the corded muscles of his throat. His lungs were afire; a red haze thickened before his eyes. The Negro leaned close, his thick lips spread in a lurid grimace that exposed yellow teeth filed to fanglike points. His hot breath, sickly-sweet with the effluvium of the drug, fanned Conan's brow.

The black's face came closer still. Now the combatants

swayed cheek to cheek, as the Kushite strove to reach
Conan's jugular vein with his fangs.

Suddenly, Conan released his grip on the Negro's
wrists, planted his palms against the other's chest, and
shoved, as once, unaided, he had pushed against the spokes
of the Wheel of Pain. His massive thews stood out in bold
relief beneath the bronzen hide of his huge arms; for long
years of toil at the Wheel had hardened them, as iron is
hardened under the hammer of the smith.

Amazement flickered across the black's visage when,
despite the enormous power of his own solid arms, he was
slowly thrust away, until his fingers slipped off the corded
muscles of his opponent's neck. In that instant, Conan
seized the black's wrists again and, bending double, pulled
the man over his back. The giant Negro flew over Conan's
shoulders to thud heavily against the packed earth.

The Kushite regained his feet almost at once. But
during that brief respite, Conan had sucked precious air into
his starved lungs. Now the two circled warily, knees bent,
legs spread, and clutching arms wide. Blood trickled down
the Cimmerian's chest from punctures in his throat made by
the black's sharpened nails. Sweat ran down his forehead
and seeped, stinging, into his eyes. He shook his head,
causing his matted mane to lift as he tried to shake the sweat
away.

Blood lust flamed in the black man's eyes. Grinning
his fanged smile, he sprang catlike at Conan. But the young
Cimmerian was ready. He twisted lightly aside and, as his
opponent flew past, brought one balled fist down on the
nape of the other's neck. Half stunned, the black fell to his
knees, while the throng yelled hoarsely. Some shouted in
amazement; others in anger, as they saw their wagers fade
away. Still others roared encouragement; for never had they
seen such a fight between an untried youth and a proven
champion.

Conan ignored the crowd. For him the world had
narrowed to one Pit and one antagonist. As the lust to kill
welled up within him, he hammered the dazed Negro again
and again, smashing his nose into a smear of red and
closing an eye with a swelling bruise.

Then the black sprang back and, bending nearly

double, hurled himself at his adversary. His bullet head slammed into Conan's belly, driving the youth back against the boards that lined the wall of the Pit. The Negro's partisans went wild with cries of "Junga! Junga!"

As Junga closed with the Cimmerian, Conan seized one ebon arm. Ignoring the pain in his belly, he wrenched that arm behind its owner's back and pulled up with all his might. The black screamed like a speared stallion as sinews tore from their moorings and the bone was twisted from its socket. He slumped to his knees, his dislocated arm hanging uselessly.

Then Conan got his hands under the black's armpits and slammed his head into the wall of the Pit. The onlookers fell silent with tension; and in the silence they heard a sound like the snapping of a stick. Conan had broken the Negro's neck. Swaying with exhaustion, Conan let the twitching body slide to the ground. He staggered away, bracing himself against the Pit wall, and gasped for air.

The crowd went mad. Chieftains ripped off golden armlets and broaches and hurled them into the Pit, at Conan's feet. But the weary Cimmerian ignored the glittering bounty. Just being alive was treasure enough for a Pit fighter.

Toghrul lowered himself into the Pit and slapped Conan's bruised and aching shoulders. The Hyrkanian grinned and gabbled incoherent praise while stooping to gather up the golden offerings.

"Come, boy!" he said at last, his hands full of gewgaws. "I always knew you would be a champion! We'll wash those cuts, and you shall have all the ale you can drink."

On unsure feet, Conan followed his owner up the ladder and into the tiring room. There Uldin awaited him with a basin of warm water, a towel, and a pitcher of cold ale.

Thus the young Cimmerian became a Pit fighter, a manslayer, battling for his life to feed the blood lust of the Nordheimers. When Toghrul found his takings dwindling in Vanaheim, he moved his people and animals eastward into

Asgard, home of the golden-haired Æsir. While the two nations hated each other and lost no opportunity to raid, plunder, and slaughter their enemies, they were united in their love of Pit fighting. It was not unusual to see tribesmen from both nations, who had busily savaged each other the month before, mingling in the Pit fight sheds, slapping backs, exchanging bear hugs, and trading toasts and wagers.

The life of a Pit fighter was not quite the worst of lives, Conan grimly discovered. To face an adversary and kill him was to enjoy, for a fleeting moment at least, the illusion of freedom. It was, in a way, to be a whole man again. The grueling torment of the Wheel had dehumanized him; the fierce battles of the Pit restored something of manhood and self-love.

Nor did Toghrul treat his favorite slaves badly. Like the owner of prized horses or dogs, his master saw that they had plenty to eat and drink: rich roasts, thick wheaten bread, and mugs of foaming black ale. Yet Toghrul took care to see that his fighters did not escape. Armed guards watched them constantly and chained them up whenever their master thought there might be a chance of their making a break.

Even more intoxicating than the strong ale, the generous portions of food, and the praise of his master, were the frenzy of the audience and the adulation of the crowd.

Conan learned that life gains an added dimension of intensity when each sunrise may be the last. After each Pit fight, he would sleep like an exhausted beast. Yet from time to time, his dreams became nightmares, in which he found himself lying, disemboweled, spilling out his guts on soil slimy with blood, while a jeering throng above spat down upon him. Then he would wake at dawn in a cold sweat, glad to find himself alive and full of vigor.

No, it was not quite the worst of lives; but the life of a Pit fighter nonetheless dulled Conan's spirit. Seeing so much of death, he became indifferent to it and cared little whether he himself lived or died, so long as the crowd greeted him with roars of lust and fury.

As the white blanket of winter settled down on Asgard, the business of Pit fighting slowed to a halt. Most of the slaves were kept occupied building huts to replace their tents; but Uldin the trainer continued to teach Conan the use of weapons other than fists, teeth, and feet. He introduced the youth to the simple staff, a six-foot length of hardwood as thick as a dog's leg, such as Conan had seen men use in his Cimmerian village. Eventually Conan graduated to the spear, using it in both hands like a quarterstaff but giving emphasis to thrusting with the metal spearhead. For such lethal practice sessions, he and Uldin wore protective padding and wielded blunt weapons.

From the spear, the Cimmerian went on to the javelin, the axe, and the sword. The first time Uldin placed a sword in Conan's hand, he turned the blade over thoughtfully. It was but a lath of iron without an edge, to which was attached an iron crossguard set into a simple wooden hilt.

"Not much of a sword," growled Conan. "Not like those my father made."

"Your father was a smith, then?"

"Aye. He knew the secret of steel. To him, steel was a gift from the gods. 'A blade of well-forged steel,' he said, 'is the only thing in the world a man can count on.' "

Uldin grunted. "The real measure of a man lies not in the steel he carries, but in himself."

"What do you mean?" asked Conan.

"In a manner of speaking, it's the *man* who is forged, not the blade. I know, for I am a forger of men. Come, take the first guard position! Raise your shield, so!"

By spring, when Toghrul pulled up stakes and moved to another section of the country, the young Cimmerian had a working knowledge of all the elementary weapons. So skillful was he in their use that he no longer flung himself on his pallet each night an aching mass of bruises from Uldin's blows and thrusts.

Yet, for all the trainer's well-intentioned discipline, Conan's lot did not grow easier. To satisfy their lust for sadistic spectacles, the Northlanders had devised many cunning ways to rip out a man's life. Sometimes Conan and his opponents fought chained together, distanced only by a girdle's length, each man being furnished with a short dirk and a firm grip on his foe's knife wrist. For variety, Toghrul and the other Pitmasters would dress their fighters as animals, encasing them in hides or furs and horned helmets in the likeness of beasts, and affixing metal claws to hands and feet.

Nor were his adversaries always men. One day Uldin told Conan, "You're to fight a Hyperborean tonight."

"What manner of folk are they?" asked Conan, who had heard vaguely that Hyperborea was a land lying east of Asgard. "I saw one once when we were both slaves of the Wheel; but we had no speech in common."

"A tall, lean, light-haired people, for the most part," said the trainer. "Dangerous foes, reputed to be wizards and sorcerers."

On this occasion, Conan and his antagonist were sent into the Pit in loincloths and sandals, with short swords in their hands and bucklers on their left arms.

Conan was amazed to discover that he faced a woman. She was slim and long-legged, and almost the height of Conan himself, who, now full-grown, towered a head above even the tall Vanir and Æsir. The woman's hair, the color of moonbeams, was woven into a thick braid, and her small breasts were bare. Although her supple body exuded an aura of sensuality, her green eyes were deathly cold. From the way she grasped her weapon, Conan sensed that she was well-practiced in her art.

The whistle blew, and the fight was on. The combatants circled warily, then engaged. Steel rang on steel and thudded against the wood and leather of the shields, the clatter resounding above the shouts of the spectators. Despite the sinewy strength in the warrior-woman's arms, Conan's musculature, toughened at the Wheel and hardened in the Pit, was decisive. For all her skill, and speed, and subtlety, Conan stolidly batted her sword aside time after time.

A heavy blow knocked the sword from the woman's hand. From the benches above rose a yell of "*Drep*! Kill!" For an instant, the woman presented a wide opening, standing immobile as if reconciled to death.

Conan hesitated. Among the compelling customs of the Cimmerians, drilled into the boy Conan, was that a man's foremost duty was to protect the women and children of the tribe. Although Cimmerians might cheerfully ambush and murder the men of another clan with whom they were at feud, deliberately to slay a woman who had done no crime was an unheard-of brutality.

Conan's hesitation lasted no longer than two heart-beats. Then the Hyperborean woman sprang back, retrieved her fallen sword, and rushed upon Conan with renewed fury. When one of her blows gashed his forehead and blood dripped into his eyes, he was hard put to defend himself.

At last, fatigue slowed the warrior-woman's attacks. Striking alternately with sword and shield, Conan beat her back against the wall of the Pit. A powerful backhand stroke split her shield and plowed into her side. As blood gushed forth, staining her white flesh, the young woman cried out and slumped to the rough dirt floor, pressing her hand against the gaping wound, as if to hold back her entrails.

Conan stepped back and glanced up. Toghrul caught his eye, pointed, and made a chopping motion with one blunt-fingered hand. When Conan still hesitated, the Pit-master repeated the unequivocal gesture with greater emphasis.

The young barbarian bent over the crumpled woman, who seemed to have lost consciousness. His sword swung up and fell in a chopping blow. Still bent, he thrust the point of his sword into the earth, grasped the blonde braid, and raised the severed head for the enjoyment of the Æsin chieftains. The crowd roared its satisfaction.

"At that moment," the king related to me, "I hated myself. Never have I told this tale before, for the deed is one of the few of which I am ashamed. True, the woman was dying, and the death I dealt her was perhaps more merciful than letting her die slowly; but still, the deed was vile and cowardly to a Cimmerian. Then I bethought me of Toghrul, who had made me thus to despise myself. All my hatred focused on him, and I swore that one day I would repay him for my shame."

The welted seam along his brow, etched by the
Hyperborean woman's sword, was only one of several that
scarred Conan's face and body during that summer in the
Pit. The barbarian youth became a good rough-and-ready,
fighter, making up in sheer strength and reach what he
lacked in the more subtle understanding of the martial arts.
But his lack of these refinements worried Toghrul. Some
day, he feared, his youthful champion would be pitted
against a swordsman of comparable strength but of superior
skills. Then Conan would be maimed or slain and, in either
case, would have no further value to the gamesman.

So, as autumn once more painted the forests red and
gold, Toghrul took his troupe far to the east, across the
bleak plains of Hyperborea to a town called Valamo, near
the farthest reaches of that land. There dwelt a master
swordsman, whom Toghrul meant to hire to teach the
Cimmerian more skillful handling of his blade. There, too,
Toghrul hoped to buy potential Pit fighters in the local slave
market; for death had thinned the troupe to half its former
number.

They made the two-month's journey in a well-guarded
caravan. At every stopping place, first the Æsir and later the
Hyperboreans gathered to admire Toghrul's champion, who
had become famous for his exploits and gigantic strength.
On these occasions, the Pitmaster, a showman to the core,
would strip the young barbarian and display him naked on a
revolving platform from which four iron chains extended
upward to the slave collar that he wore. Nordheimers and
their women gladly paid their copper coins to stare with
curious, appraising eyes at Conan's magnificent physique.

Conan returned their stares with stolid indifference. He
guessed that it would have amused them to witness the
arousal of his body by the seductive smiles and sidelong
glances of the women; but he was determined to deny them
even this small pleasure. He hated them all.

At Valamo, on the distant borders of Hyrkania, the
master swordsman, a Hyrkanian named Oktar, imparted his
secrets to the Cimmerian. All through the winter, the youth
drilled and practiced under Oktar's direction. By the time

spring melted winter's heavy snows, Toghrul was satisfied that nothing remained to teach his champion.

During his stay, Conan learned much about these eastern lands of which he had heard only the scantiest of rumors. As Toghrul's most favored Pit fighter, he was often allowed to spend the evening hours in the Pitmaster's yurt, when his master entertained the warlords and chieftains who drifted into Valamo from time to time to buy and sell or to trade gossip. Sometimes Toghrul was honored by the presence of Turanians, men of Hyrkanian stock who had drawn ahead of their nomadic fellows in the arts and sciences of civilization, and who, on the western shores of the Vilayet Sea, had reared glittering cities and learned the ways of urban life.

Most of the time, Conan sat cross-legged and silent on the carpeted floor of his master's yurt. But when opportunity arose, he would ply these strangers with questions about methods of organized warfare. His questions amused the war leaders, who thought the principles of strategy and tactics of little use to a mere Pit slave, whose fate it was to fight a single adversary again and again, until death overtook him.

Yet Conan realized that the more he knew of matters such as these, the better would be his chances of survival. He began to think ahead. He would not, he resolved, be a Pit slave forever. Since the world appeared to be a place of constant conflict, where the strong took whatever they had the power to take, he would learn to do likewise.

On one occasion, after rolling up the large hide map that he had spread out across the carpet, it pleased a Hyrkanian general to query those who sat late in Toghrul's yurt over cups of fine white wine.

"What is the best thing in life?" he asked a Turanian princeling, resplendent in silken trousers and boots of scarlet leather strapped in silver.

Gems sparkled in the lamplight as the Turanian spread his hands in a graceful gesture. "The good life is on the open steppe, under a clear sky, with a fleet horse between your knees, a well-trained falcon on your wrist, and a cold, fresh wind in your hair."

The general shook his head and smiled. "Wrong, Highness! What say you to this, Khitaian?"

He shot the question at a small, elderly man who had spoken little. Conan understood that the man had come from a land called Khitai, a year's journey to the east. The small man had a wrinkled, parchment-yellow skin, stretched over a flat, slant-eyed face. He huddled in his quilted robes, which were drawn tightly to protect his thin frame from the evening's chill. Slowly, he murmured, "I say that life is best when a man can boast a love of learning, and has acquired wisdom and an appreciation for fine poetry."

Again the general shook his head. Then he caught the intense gaze of Conan, who sat cross-legged on a low, circular dais in the center of the yurt, clad in a warm tunic, but chained as before. With ill-concealed amusement, the Hyrkanian general asked, "What says the young barbarian giant in answer to my question?"

Conan's mouth twitched in a shadow of a smile as he replied, "The best of life is to confront your enemy face to face, to see his hot blood spill upon the earth, and to hear the lamentations of his women!"

Approval lit the dark eyes of the general. "The Pit has not broken the spirit of your champion, O Toghrul. Neither has it sapped his will. Beware lest this young tiger some day turn and rend you!"

"He wears chains so that he cannot," said Toghrul, chuckling.

Conan said nothing more; but a strange volcanic fire smoldered briefly in his fierce blue eyes.

With the coming of spring, Toghrul gathered his people and horses for another trek. This time he headed into the west wind, back across Hyperborea to the lands of the Æsir and Vanir. Once again he had a full complement of Pit fighters; and he looked forward to a profitable season among the Nordheimers.

At length the caravan stopped at the village of Kolari, a mere crossroads encampment. Here, in the lone tavern, traders from near and far rested before continuing on across the steppes and tundras. Kolari lay in a region of rolling hills; and in a hillside cave, Toghrul found a place to keep and exploit his champion during his few days' halt. The cave had once been the abode of a holy hermit, who had brought to it some amenities and, to deter unwanted petitioners, had fitted a door of iron bars across the entrance. To make the place more comfortable, Toghrul added wall hangings and cushions from his own yurt. He locked the Cimmerian within; and for hours every day he stood outside collecting fees from people who wished to gaup at his famous Pit-fighting champion.

One evening at sunset, the curious departed for their evening meal. Conan, his massive physique contrasting sharply with the dainty comfort of his furnishings, sat with his back to the wall of the cave, trying by candlelight to decipher the words on a scroll. He had picked up a smattering of written Hyrkanian; now, with knotted brow, slowly moving his lips, he was puzzling out each word written in the spidery script of Turan. The writing on the scroll was a love poem, which mightily perplexed the youth even when he understood most of the words. He had never before heard sentiments like these.

Presently, Toghrul's raised voice drew his attention. The Pitmaster was chaffering with a slim young woman wrapped in a cloak of fine sable. Her dress, jewels, and confident manner suggested a lady of high rank, perhaps even kin to royalty. As Conan caught the exchange of words, he gathered that the woman wished to retain his services as a love partner for the night. He drew a sharp breath in amazement, for such a thing was unheard-of among the Cimmerian tribesmen. Then his astonishment changed to ire at the thought of his master's gaining riches from such a use of his slave's body.

Toghrul took the girl's money, unlocked the gate, opened it just enough for her to slip through, then hastily relocked it. As the girl, dropping her fur cloak, approached him hesitantly, the Cimmerian's eyes roved up and down her slender, diaphanously clad form. He felt his blood pound as he stepped forward to meet her. Then he noticed Toghrul at the gate, grinning, his eyes ashine in the candlelight.

"What are you waiting for?" growled Conan.

"To see your performance, Cimmerian," snickered the Pitmaster.

"To the nine hells with you!" snarled Conan. "There'll be no performance so long as you stand there goggling!"

The girl spoke in a light, high voice. "Indeed, sirrah, I have paid you well. Now depart, I command you!"

As Toghrul, disappointed, shrugged and strode off, Conan said, "Now, lady, you will have to show me a thing or two. I have had some experience at manslaying, but this kind of combat is new to me. . . ."

The full moon was on its downward path across the heavens when a small sound broke Conan's slumber. He raised himself on one elbow, staring through the darkness. A faint light came from the declining moon, which shot silvern arrows through the imprisoning bars. As a lazy cloud drifted across the moon, the landscape seemed bathed in lusterless crimson. A heavy silence lay upon the world, as if Nature held her breath and waited. Beside Conan, the sleeping girl stirred.

The Cimmerian did not know what had aroused him; but his savage instincts warned him of impending danger. Quietly, he reached for his garments and pulled them on.

Somewhere a dog barked, then another. Soon every dog within earshot gave uneasy tongue. A hoarse whinnied; then Conan heard a chorus of whinnies. Asses brayed, and restless cattle lowed in their pastures. The entire animal kingdom seemed to cry out a warning of impending disaster.

Suddenly the earth shook. A muffled moan within the ground swelled to a rumbling roar. The ground cracked open. A stream of rocks cascaded down the hillside past the entrance to the cave.

The girl woke, screaming, and fumbled for her lover; but Conan, fully clad, was crouching on the cave floor, his outstretched arms braced against the stone wall, as the ground heaved and shook beneath him. Huddled there, he recalled the legends that his father told him about giants in the earth and wondered whether some of them, astir, were causing the catastrophe.

The rumble increased in volume, until Conan had to

shout to the trembling girl, urging her to join him. From Kolari came a continuing ululation of screams as terror-stricken people rushed from their tumbling houses. Behind Conan and the girl, a section of the cave roof collapsed with a thunderous roar, filling the air with rock dust.

As Conan, growling curses, seized the bars that penned them in, the ground beneath his feet split open. A line like black lightning zigzagged down the rock in which the hinges of the barred gate were set. The gate loosened in Conan's desperate grip, as the lower hinge parted from its setting. A violent push, and the gate hung awry.

"Get out, girl!" shouted Conan, as he forced the gate ajar. The girl squeezed past him through the narrow opening and ran screaming into the night, clutching her furs and flimsy garments against her naked bosom.

With another mighty heave, Conan broke the gate loose from its remaining hinge and hurled it down the hillside. As the earth rocked and vibrated beneath his feet, he staggered out into the moonlight and glared wildly at the scene of devastation. In the middle distance, he perceived the houses of Kolari in ruins, and their homeless tenants running aimlessly about, like ants after the obliteration of their nest.

"Conan!" came the voice of Toghrul. "Conan! Help me!"

Below him, at the foot of the little hill, Conan saw the Pitmaster's head protruding from a wide crack in the earth. He saw that the earth had opened beneath the Hyrkanian's feet and swallowed him to his shoulders. Wedged in the crack, the man was unable to free himself.

"Pull me out!" implored the Pitmaster.

"Why should I?"

"I'll pay gold! I'll give you your freedom! Only save me now!"

"My freedom, eh?" Conan threw back his head and laughed—his first good laugh since the Vanir had captured him, ten long years ago. "That I already have. Stay there, swine! If the earth swallows you down, good riddance to you!"

Conan turned and walked away. Guided by the moonlight, he headed for a clump of trees on a hillock in the distance. He had neither supplies nor weapons and did not know whither he was going, but at least he knew that southward the weather was warmer. Behind him, Toghrul's frantic voice rose to an awful shriek as, in a final earth tremor, the crack that held him closed once more.

Conan saw no one, alive or dead, in the direction he chose to travel, save, after a time, one Hyrkanian warrior, who sprawled beneath a fallen tree. In its descent, the tree had broken the fellow's back. Conan knelt and looted the corpse for such articles as he might need: boots, flint and steel, a dagger, a fur cloak, and a bag of coins. He also took the man's quiver and bow case, although he looked doubtfully at them for the bow was little used among the Cimmerians, and Conan had never learned to shoot.

"You'll have no use for these in the red pits of Hell, Hyrkanian," he said cheerfully, "and they may serve me well before I join you there." So saying, he donned the dead man's gear and glided away through the trees.

Then, as the first faint glow of dawn suffused the eastern sky, Conan increased his pace and headed south.

IV

The Witch

The plain stretched southward under a pewter sky. Here and there the ground showed black where winds had scoured away the snow, exposing naked earth.

Once more Conan paused in his trudging to glance back along the path that he had traveled. Straining his ears, he heard the telltale whining and knew that wolves were still on his trail. From the distance came their eerie song. He scowled, set his jaw, and gathered his bearskin cloak about him. If only, in all this bleak, flat stretch of land, he could find a rocky place to shield him—something to put his back against—he could face the pack and use his dagger to good advantage.

Grimly, the Cimmerian turned to plod ahead; but in the dull, metallic luminescence of the motionless mist, he could not see his surroundings clearly. He strode along, nevertheless, his keen barbarian eyes searching for a haven against the hungry fangs. At last he found one. It was only a low rise, a wrinkle in the earth's skin; but the higher ground was strewn with boulders. On the crest of this small rise, he hoped to make his stand; for there the beasts could come at him only singly, or at the worst in pairs.

As he began to clamber up the rocky pile, his booted feet slipped on the sheathing ice. A cold wind came up and tugged at his cloak as if to hold him back. Still he persevered and made some progress. Pausing to catch his breath at last, he turned to see a dozen gaunt, dark-furred forms lope into view. The wolves' eyes burned like glowing coals through the gathering murk, as the gray light faded from the clouded heavens.

Seeing their quarry trying to escape, the pack broke into a chorus of snarls. Just before the foremost reached the foot of the rock pile, Conan found a smooth, upright slab which thrust up from the side of the knoll. In shape it was oddly symmetrical, as though hewn by artisans of some forgotten race and set there for a marker. Conan neither knew or cared about that; the slab was something he could stand against, something to protect his back.

Whining and growling, the wolves threaded a passage between the boulders, scrambling for footholds as they clawed their way up the rough hillside. One leaped high in the air to snap at the Cimmerian's leg, but a slash of his dirk caught the beast across its muzzle. With a yelp of pain, it fell back, giving its prey a moment's respite.

As he inched along the ledge that fronted the vertical slab, in search of a more secure footing, Conan's fingers found a narrow gap in the rock. A quick glance revealed a dark opening, just wide enough for a man to slip through sidewise. Once within the sheltering cleft, however small the space, he knew that he would gain an advantage against his pursuers.

Lithe as a panther, Conan wriggled through the slot in the stone; but his cloak caught on a jagged rock and was torn from his shoulders. Through the aperture, he watched the wolves hurl themselves upon the fur, their fangs ripping the bear's hide to ribbons.

For some reason that he could not fathom, the animals did not even try to squirm through the opening. From the way they whined and scratched against the slab, he sensed that, starving though they were, they feared to pass through this mysterious stone portal.

Turning, Conan found himself in a larger space than he had expected, a stone-walled cubicle with a flat, stone-paved floor. The regularity of the floor and walls gave the barbarian youth an uneasy premonition that the chamber had been fashioned by intelligent beings, human or otherwise. He felt his way in the dark along the smooth wall and came to an opening through which a flight of smoothly-chiseled stone steps descended into deeper darkness. He followed them to their foot.

On the lower level, the floor seemed littered with debris, rotted cloth intermixed with hard lumps that he could not at first identify. He gathered up a handful of the unseen litter, wondering if it were combustible. He felt in his pouch for the flint and steel he had taken from the dead Hyrkanian. Soon he had a small flame burning, for the cloth was dry and ignited easily.

By this feeble orange light, Conan saw that the walls were embellished with polished stone reliefs, an intricate mixture of bizarre figures and forms unknown to him. Examining the floor, he found it cluttered with skulls and bones, the remains of at least a score of human beings. He saw that the bones were clean and dry, the flesh having long since disintegrated into dust.

Peering deeper into the gloom, Conan discovered a huge throne, carved from a block of some opalescent material such as marble or alabaster. On this seat of honor sat an enormous skeletal warrior, still clad in copper armor of a strange design, turned green by the corrosion of many years. Conan guessed that the living man whose bones these were had been half again as tall as he, perhaps a member of a long-forgotten race.

Lighting his way with a rude torch fashioned from a femur wrapped in a piece of rotting cloth, Conan approached the armed figure. Beneath the shadow of the heavy helm, the face of the skull seemed frozen in a silent scream. Across the spread knees of the armored skeleton lay a great sword, sheathed in leather so rotted that patches of iron beneath the hide were visible. The hilt and pommel of corroded bronze crawled with cryptic characters, wrought by a master's hand.

Conan took up the sword. At the touch of his fingers, the scabbard crumbled into dust and thin fragments of bronze fell to the floor with the ghost of a tinkle. The blade, now fully exposed, proved to be a huge length of dull iron, spotted with patches of corrosion; but rust had not bitten it deeply enough to affect its strength. The edge, when Conan thumbed it, was still sharp.

Conan's eyes clouded with painful memories as he caressed the perfect planes of the blade and the exquisite workmanship of the hilt. He recalled the making of the great steel sword that was his father's masterpiece. Shrugging the memory away, Conan hefted the ancient weapon. Heavy as it was, he found the balance so perfect that it seemed made for his arm alone. He raised the sword above his head, and felt his thews swell with power and his heart beat faster with the pride of possession. With such a blade, no destiny would be too high for a warrior to aspire to! With such a blade, even a barbarian slave, a Pit fighter scorned and marked for death, might hack his way to an honored place among the rulers of the earth.

Exhilarated by the dreams that the splendid weapon aroused in his barbarian breast, Conan feinted and cut the air with wild abandon; and as the keen sword sliced through the stale air of the death chamber, he uttered the venerable war cry of the Cimmerians. Loud and clear he shouted it; and the cry reverberated around the chamber, disturbing ancient shadows and age-old dust. In his exuberance, the young barbarian never paused to think that such a challenge, wide-flung in such a place, might rouse thoughts and feelings that had slumbered there for countless centuries among the bones of those whose thoughts they were.

Suddenly, Conan heard an answering war cry. It seemed to come from a great distance, carried on the wind. But there was no wind. Conan paused, his sword arm still upraised. Was it perhaps the wolves that howled? Again the mad cry rose, so near now that it beat against his ears and deafened him. Conan wheeled. He felt the hair lift from his scalp and his blood congeal to ice. For the dead man lived and moved.

Slowly, the skeleton rose from the marble throne, glaring at the Cimmerian youth from the deep pits now filled, it seemed, with demonic fire. Bone rubbed against bone, like tree branches brushing together in a storm, as the terrible grinning skull approached on funereal feet. Conan, his arm still raised, stood frozen by horror into immobility.

Suddenly a bony claw shot out, to snatch the sword from Conan's hand. Numb with terror, Conan retreated step by step. Only the Cimmerian's labored breath and the clicking of bones against the stone floor of the chamber broke the silence.

Now the dead thing had Conan backed against a wall. Pit fighter though he was, ready to do battle with man or beast and fearing neither pain nor mortal foes, he was still a barbarian and like all barbarians he feared the terrors of the grave and the monstrous beings that inhabit the dark world and the hells beneath hells. The small torch burned low as he stood paralyzed by fear. Then a wolf howled.

Galvanized into action by that familiar sound, Conan's terror melted like the snow in spring. He brought the sword down with a chopping blow that lopped off the clutching bony claw. He swiveled to the side and, in the sputtering light, searched vainly for the stairs down which he had come. Relentlessly, the helmeted skull strode forward. With swift, powerful strokes Conan defended himself. At last he found the narrow stairs, and backing up a single step, he drove his weapon through the rusted armor, through the bare rib cage, into the area where a living heart would beat.

With a sigh like sedge blown by an autumn wind, the walking skeleton paused in mid-step. The giant form reeled, took two tottering steps towards the throne, and collapsed into a heap of bones and dust. The helmet rang like a cracked bell when it struck the stone flooring. Then the torch flickered and went out.

For a moment, the Cimmerian stood staring into the darkness, unable to comprehend that his supernatural adversary was truly dead and that the great sword was his. Then he turned and, holding his weapon at the ready, mounted the stairs.

At last Conan emerged into the moonlight to find the wolves still waiting for him. Howling, they bounded toward him, tongues lolling from their fanged jaws. With a tight smile, he took his stance on the ledge and raised the long blade over his head. As the first beast hurled itself toward him, Conan pivoted, sweeping his sword in a horizontal arc. Caught in mid-leap, the wolf was tossed high in the air and fell, yelping, to its death on the boulders.

Before the Cimmerian could lift his sword arm to deliver another slashing blow, a second wolf sprang at him, its jaws agape. In the white light of the moon, he drove the point of his blade between the open jaws, seating it deep in the animal's gullet. The wolf's legs scrambled frantically on the rounded surface of a boulder as it tried in vain to tear itself loose from the impaling blade.

At that instant, a third wolf dove at Conan from the side, snapping at his legs. Still encumbered by the spitted animal, Conan kicked out, in time to catch the new attacker on its nose. The beast drew back with a yelp, then made another dive; but Conan, having freed his sword, dealt the attacker a blow that laid open its skull.

With three of their number down, the remaining wolves drew back. Whining, they trotted off, tails low, and disappeared into the low-lying mists.

Conan spent the night, a long and wearisome time, hidden among the boulders on the upland, alert to the twin dangers of further attacks by hungering beasts or by walking dead men from the nearby cave. In the gray dawn, he skinned the three dead wolves and, tying the skins together, made a crude mantle for protection against the cold. Some of the flesh he roasted over a small fire and ate with ravenous enjoyment; some he wrapped in the skin of a wolf's leg to assuage his hunger during the journey southward.

The sword Conan slung on his back, thrust through the dead soldier's belt and secured there by a string of animal sinews. Thus outfitted and provisioned, he clambered down the rock pile and, sighting on a pallid sun, headed south.

Three days later, the level tundra had given way to a vista of gently rolling hills crowned with scrub timber. The ground beneath his feet had grown soft from the melting of the lingering snows, and clear water ran in rills from tunnels in the thawing drifts. In the distance, a lazy pillar of smoke wavered upward to meet the high overcast.

Conan headed for the place whence the smoke ascended; and, coming to a clearing, found a stone-walled, sod-roofed dwelling dug into the side of a hill. Curiously carved wooden poles jutted from the earth at crazy angles about the hut, like a flimsy palisade. Several standing stones had been rudely chipped into the semblance of human heads, grimacing or shouting into the uncaring wind. His primitive instincts attuned to the supernatural, Conan could almost feel the emanations of evil power arising from these cryptic sticks and stones.

The door of the hut stood ajar, and the barbarian approached it, moving with the feline caution of a stalking leopard. Suddenly he stopped, rigid with amazement; for, tethered by a chain to a heavy stone post, he saw a crouching figure, wrapped in ragged furs. It was a man, squat, bowlegged, and half naked, who with the eyes of an injured animal regarded the newcomer. Voiceless and unmoving as the stone against which he huddled, the short man stared at the young Cimmerian from slitted, ebon eyes.

Suddenly, a voice, as clear as a cowbell in the gloaming, jolted Conan from his curious contemplation.

"There is warmth in fire." The voice was soft and inviting.

Conan raised his eyes to see a woman's figure silhouetted against the firelight from her hearth. Her curvaceous body, pressed against the portal of her home, radiated a sinister but inviting mystery; her languid, smiling eyes ran down the strong body of the Cimmerian youth, exuding an eroticism as strong as a caress.

"Do you not wish to warm yourself by my fire?" Her face, framed by her long black hair, was past the bloom of youth, but there was a compelling beauty in it that was as old as time.

Conan, restrained by his premonition of evil, hesitated for a heartbeat, while the woman, with a secret smile, turned from the doorway to stoke her fire of tamarisk chips. Drawn by her easy manner and the glow of her oval face in the firelight, Conan ducked under the low lintel and entered the hut.

The fire leaped up, and by its roseate glow, Conan studied the room. The stone walls were enhanced by hangings of animal hides; the floor was covered by skins of luxuriant softness but of beasts unfamiliar to the Cimmerian. Strange skulls were suspended from the twin posts that supported the sod roof—bears with great teeth, saber-fanged cats, and one-horned beasts of indescribable immensity.

Before the fire the woman spread a low table with a wooden platter of barley bread and goat cheese, a bowl of dried fruit, and a mug of fresh milk. Then she beckoned to him, and gratefully he settled down to enjoy the repast. Sated, he looked up to find the woman leaning against the nearer centerpost, studying him. An expression of amusement curled her full-lipped mouth.

"From the north, that is whence you come," she said in her throaty voice.

Suddenly aware that the woman has been staring at him, Conan looked down, uneasy. His hand dropped to the sword now lying by his side.

"I am a Cimmerian," he said.

The woman, noting the youth's ardent glance and evident embarrassment, laughed harshly. "You are a slave! Do you not think that I can see a slave by his eyes? Barbarian slave!"

There was an uneasy silence. Then, with a sinuous movement, the woman tossed back her long hair and prowled about the room with unsettling, erotic grace. Something about her shadow, not quite where it should be, disturbed the barbarian youth.

"Where do you go, Cimmerian?" she demanded.

Conan shrugged. "To the south."

"Why?" she persisted, smiling, a touch of cruelty in her expression.

Conan threw her a brief glance. "They say it is warmer there, and they ask few questions of strangers. Besides, there is gold to be earned by a man who can use a sword."

The woman bent over the fire and threw a powder into the hot coals. Suddenly the flames roared up, then fell away. She studied the surge of flame, her lips curling, then said:

"Gold, women, thievery—that's civilization! What would a savage like you know of civilized life? But it matters not. In a short time your spine will be nailed to a tree."

The woman poured the barbarian a cup of wine, then stood staring at him with rising sexual interest. Under her soft robe, her voluptuous breasts rose and fell, as her breathing quickened. A strange light shone in the depths of her dark eyes, and the firelight glistened on her firm, oiled limbs as she rubbed her hands against her thighs with rising excitement.

Acutely aware of the woman's desires, Conan looked into his wine cup. The surface of the liquid gleamed like polished silver. Then, as Conan drank deeply of the dark wine, his manhood responded to the lust she radiated. Still, he distrusted her. He could not have told why, save that there were strange things about her and about the place in which she lived. He noted the smile, which suddenly became a frozen mask, drained of all entrancing warmth. And the eyes, which lost, for a moment only, all humanity.

"They said you would come . . ." She spoke in a sibilant whisper, while her eyes, phosphorescent in the firelight, were fixed upon him. "From the north, they said . . . a man of great strength. A conqueror, a humbler of kings, who would one day seize a throne for himself and hold it against the red tides of war and treachery. One who would crush the serpents of the earth beneath his sandaled feet. . . ."

"Serpents? Did you say serpents?" Conan's voice was razor-sharp, and his glance was keen upon her.

She returned look for look. "What seek you in the south, barbarian? Speak truth, now."

"A standard . . . on a shield, perhaps, or on a banner. There are two serpents, face to face; yet they are one, joined at the tail." He clenched his fists, remembering.

"Upholding a black sun, with ebon rays," the woman added, nodding.

"You know whereof I speak?" Conan moved forward, grasping the woman by her upper arms. She slid out of his grasp, her shadow not quite keeping up with her.

"I know. But there is a price, barbarian."

"Name it," growled the Cimmerian.

A smile curved her full lips as, arms spread wide, she moved towards him. Conan's blood surged within him as he took her into the circle of his arms and felt her breasts and thighs pressed against him. She fumbled in her excitement to loosen her garments and his; and, all thoughts of resistance vanquished, he gave himself over to the ecstasy of her passion.

Their naked bodies glistened in the firelight, as she writhed against him, her breath hot with desire; Conan responded in an impassioned blend of need and pain. All thought vanished in the intensity of his emotion. He felt her fingers clawing at his back and stroking his unruly hair, but his passion absorbed him utterly. As he neared his climax, a faint moan sounded in the woman's throat. She whispered a message, no less ferocious than her love-making.

"In Shadizar of Zamora, the crossroads of the world, you will find that which you seek. But you would be a fool to go. . . . Only fools seek their own death. . . ."

Then, convulsed in a violent orgasm, she took her ultimate pleasure of him, and he of her.

Something, he did not know what, caused him to open his eyes a heartbeat later. A revulsion of horror replaced the passion of the earlier moment.

"Crom!" he breathed.

For, even as he watched the woman in his arms, her white teeth lengthened into fangs, like those of a wolf. Her lips and nipples turned an iridescent blue, and the fingers that clutched his shoulders became flesh-searing claws, like the talons of some monstrous, predatory bird. A dark smoke rose in serpentine wisps from nostrils set in a burgeoning snout, and the tongue that darted out was the forked tongue of a serpent.

Conan, still locked in an embrace of love, found himself enveloped in the unrelenting arms of death. He struggled to free himself from the hideous thing that wound limbs of iron about him, like the coils of a giant snake. And when her eyelids lifted, he found himself confronting the slit-pupiled orbs of no earthly woman. All his strength, he realized, could not free him from the fate that awaited him.

Then he remembered his training in the Pit and the wrestling tricks Uldin had taught him. While the demon-woman clutched him closer, Conan ceased to struggle. Suddenly, he twisted and rolled with her toward the fire, thrusting her scaled, inhuman back against the burning coals. Her long locks, which seemed to have developed a serpentine life of their own, hissed as they burst into flame.

Shrieking, the monster strove to rise from the dancing flames; then it shrank and blackened while jets of colored fire exploded into whirling sparks. From the incinerated body, a weightless fireball arose and spun around the chamber, shedding a momentary radiance on the hanging hides and skulls of animals. The door burst open, as if from the pressure of an unseen hand, and the fireball careened out into the darkness. A dwindling spark, like a shooting star, quickly vanished into the distance. With it a lingering cry of agony faded into nothingness.

Bathed in cold sweat and weak from the release of tension, the young Cimmerian sank to his knees and began groping for his clothing.

"Crom!" he exclaimed, and followed the word with a curse.

The stench of burning flesh was swept from the room by the night wind that poured in through the open door. The hearth fire sank to a bed of smoldering coals.

As Conan went to close the door against the chill wind and the evil things that infest the dark hours, his eye fell upon the huddled being whose alert gaze reflected the red glow of the fire. Enscorcelled by the witch-woman, Conan had completely forgotten the miserable creature, who now regarded him inscrutably.

"Food!" the prisoner croaked. "I starve, barbarian! I've had no food for days."

"Who says you'll have some now?" scowled Conan. "What are you doing here?"

"I'm dinner for the wolves, pets of the witch-woman. She put a spell on me and bound me here. Just leave me food, so I may have the strength, when the wolves come, to die fighting like a man."

"Who are you?" rumbled Conan.

The small man rose and faced Conan with a dignity that belied his misery and his rags. "I am Subotai, a Hyrkanian of the Kerlait tribe. In happier days, an archer, an assassin, and a thief."

Conan studied the Hyrkanian. He was small and as lean as a ferret. His set of head and shoulders reflected stealth and cunning, hard-bitten courage, and an honesty that Conan found to his liking. Here, he thought, is a man who might throw a lie in your face but would never stab you in the back.

As beady black eyes watched hopefully, Conan searched the hut, located the keys and, by the light of the rising moon, unlocked the shackles. The little man grinned crookedly as he staggered toward the open door, rubbing his unshackled limbs.

Conan waved him in. "Eat and drink," he growled.

While Subotai gnawed on the remains of Conan's supper and guzzled the wine, the Cimmerian prowled around the hut, selecting things that he might need and things that pleased him: a silver-mounted belt, a sheath for his sword, gem-studded wristlets, a pendant carved in a strange design, and a hooded cloak of heavy fur to replace the untanned wolf skins, which had begun to stink.

Dawn was a pale gleam across the vast reaches of the treeless plain, as Conan threw open the door of the witch's cabin to watch the break of day. Silver light glinted on a thin blanket of new-fallen snow, snow that would melt in the sun's warmth but now wrapped the bare earth in the shell-pink mantle of a queen. The barbarian youth, breathing the clear air, was eager to be gone from this place of vile enchantments. He turned to his companion who sat, hugging his knees, beside the embers.

"Now that you are free, whither do you go?" he asked.

"To Zamora," the Hyrkanian replied, grinning. "The capital, Shadizar, is a city of thieves, and thievery is my business."

"You told me that you were a man of war," said Conan, looking at the small man keenly.

"I come from a race of generals. The essence of warfare is deception; so I learn the way by practicing the art of theft." Subotai, black eyes sparkling, looked up at Conan with his crooked smile.

"An unhealthy profession, so they say."

"And what do you do, Cimmerian?"

"I am a slayer of men."

Subotai's laugh rang against the stone walls of the hut. "More sanguine than thievery, to be sure. But of a more limited future. Thieves seldom get caught and, if they are, get beaten; but murderers are crucified."

"Then why were you trussed up out here for wolfbait?"

"I did not know it was a witch from whom I tried to steal. She caught me in the web of her enchantments, as she did you. Now, thanks to you, I have no need to steal."

Conan, restive, lingered at the door, while Subotai rummaged among the witch's things, plucking a fur garment from a chest, choosing a bow and quiver of arrows to his liking, and strapping a scabbarded curved sword to his belt. Conan watched with approval as the Mongol swept the remaining food into a sack and slung the bag across his shoulder.

They left the hut together. Ahead of them lay rolling hills, bright-crested with dawn's liquid gold, and smudged, here and there, where scrub oaks, black and gaunt, broke through the thin blanket of snow.

"I, too, am bound southwards for Zamora," Conan said briefly.

"Then shall we go together?" suggested Subotai. "It is good to have a friend at your back when trouble comes."

Conan looked down at the small man at his side and shrugged. "Do you know the road to Zamora?"

Subotai nodded.

Conan shouldered his gear. "Then let's be on our way."

V

The Priestess

The journey to Shadizar of Zamora was long and weary. Above the travelers stretched the vast emptiness of the firmament, deep blue by day, and cloudless, in these climes; by night a canopy of black velvet upon which the prodigal gods had stitched handfuls of diamonds.

Below their feet lay a seldom-traveled track, which snaked across the flat prairie and the rondure of patient hills. Here the naked black soil flaunted its shabby finery of withered grasses, like some swarthy strumpet, past her prime. Scrub vegetation alone broke the eternal monotony of the steppe, that source of man's wide migration.

Conan and Subotai strode through this empty land with a measured pace that devoured the leagues, the small man often trotting to keep up with the limber strides of the giant Cimmerian. Sometimes they ran. Conan would lope along, with the Hyrkanian pounding at his side.

Once, as they rested, Conan growled, "You have strong legs for one so small, and lungs like a smith's bellows."

Subotai grinned. "To follow the profession of a thief, a man must learn to outrun his enemies."

During the fortnight on the road, they came to rich forest lands where stands of trees stood tall beside lakes and ponds gouged eons before by the feet of glaciers. They crossed a low pass and descended to the banks of the Nezvaya River. The stream ran south before turning east at the Zamorian border; and the adventurers followed its banks.

When the provisions brought from the witch's house gave out, they had to spend part of each day foraging for food. Conan speared fish in the river with a crude spear whittled from a sapling, while Subotai prowled the forest with his arrow nocked. One day he would bring in a hare; the next, a badger. Some days they went to sleep hungry.

In time the forest lands thinned out, save for a gallery of trees along the Nezvaya. Wide meadows lay before them, splashed with the amber, vermilion, and cornflower blue of early spring flowers. Smiling skies, sun-flecked, announced the unmourned passing of the winter cold.

When Subotai's arrow brought down a wild ass, the companions spent the day smoking the meat, so that they could go forward for several days without further stops. As they lounged by the crackling fire, over which hung strips and slabs of drying flesh, Conan put aside his natural taciturnity to learn more about the steppe-dweller and his people.

"To what gods do your people pray?" he asked.

The Hyrkanian shrugged. "I pray to the Four Winds, which rule the land. The Winds of Heaven bring the snow, the rain, the odor of the beasts we hunt, and the sound of approaching enemies. Tell me, Cimmerian, what gods are in the prayers of your people?"

"Crom, father of stars, king of gods and men," answered Conan gruffly; for he little liked to dwell on such matters. "But my people seldom pray to him; I, never. Crom is aloof in his high heaven, indifferent to the needs and prayers of mortals."

"Does this god of yours reward your sins with punishments?"

Conan chuckled. "He cares not about the sins of puny men."

"What good, then, is a god who pays no heed to prayers and fails to punish errors?"

"When I go down the long road that leads to Crom's

great throne, he'll ask one question of me: Have I solved the riddle of my life? And if I cannot answer, he will drive me forth to wander the empty heavens, a homeless ghost. For Crom is hard and strong and will endure forever."

Subotai said eagerly, "My gods serve men. They help us in our hour of need."

Conan glowered. "Crom is master of your Four Winds," he growled as if to give himself conviction. "He drives them as a man drives the horses of a chariot."

The small man shrugged, too sleepy, or perhaps too wise, to continue a fruitless argument.

Some days later, as stars began to wink in the twilight, Conan and Subotai reached the border of Zamora. In that darkling land of shadowed secrets, furtive spies, profound philosophers, depraved kings, and sloe-eyed women, each traveler hoped to find that which he sought: Conan, the meaning of the twisted snakes upholding a black sun; Subotai, wealth that could be his for the taking.

"Zamora!" sighed Subotai, gesturing broadly. "South lies Zamora. The land to the west is Brythunia, while if you follow the river eastward a few leagues, you enter the territory of Turan. In Zamora cross all the caravans of the world, laden with the riches of distant kingdoms: superb carpets from Iranistan, spiced fruits from Turan, the famed pearls of Kosala, gems from the iron hills of Vendhya, and the heady wines of Shem.

"Ah, my barbarian friend, here is civilization—ancient, wicked, steeped in splendid sin. Have you tasted the pleasures of civilization, Conan of Cimmeria, or seen its lofty towers and teeming bazaars?"

"Not yet," said Conan curtly. "Let us get to that border town before nightfall and waste no further time on words."

Subotai shrugged. "Rhetoric, I see, is an art unknown to the folk of Cimmeria."

The frontier town of Yazdir presented a façade of stone houses with thatched roofs, surrounded by a wall two man-heights high. Outside the wall, a clutter of barns, sties, pens, and corrals housed a multitude of livestock. A pair of mail-clad guards at the gate were too engrossed in a game of dice to look up as the two adventurers passed them.

Although the streets were little more than noisome, muddy alleys, to the young barbarian they seemed far more impressive than the crooked lanes of his native village, or even than the thoroughfares of the little towns of Nordheim and Hyperborea. The center square of Yazdir was paved with flagstones, and around it were set several larger buildings. As Conan gawked, Subotai pointed out the temple, the barracks, the courthouse, the inn, and large houses which he guessed to be the mansions of local magnates.

In the square, merchants of a score of nations hawked exotic wares. Some were packing up their merchandise to close their stalls for the night; others were still in full cry. Conan bought a round loaf and a sausage and munched them as he strolled about, eyeing the dazzling assortment of weapons, garments, jewelry, slaves, and such humble goods as farm implements and cooking pots.

Everywhere he looked, Conan saw marvels: gaudy mountebanks with trained monkeys and dancing bears; painted courtesans, both male and female; a troupe of slant-eyed acrobats from some unknown sunrise land; a bookseller who swore his codices contained the wisdom of the ages. Magicians in wooden booths performed miracles for pence. Solemn astrologers offered horoscopes and forecasts of things to come. Stout merchants displayed fine woollen rugs, lustrous fabrics, and trays of rings and bracelets, while deformed beggars thrust wooden bowls beneath the noses of the travelers, and starveling boys capered in mock merriment for pennies.

Entranced, Conan and his companion meandered past pens and cages housing strange animals: yaks, camels, and a snow leopard. They continued on into a street where, with musical clangor, smiths worked copper, brass, silver, and iron. Around a corner, they found workers tooling leather and offering displays of shoes, boots, belts, scabbards, saddles, harness, and leather-bound coffers.

From time to time, Conan paused before one stall or another to ask, "Do you know aught of a design of two serpents intertwined and facing each other, with a black sun between?"

Sometimes the merchant addressed had no knowledge of the Hyrkanian tongue, and the Cimmerian had not yet learned the language of Zamora. Sometimes the reply was obsequious. "Nay, young master, I have not. But I have goblets of true Shemitish glass, made from the pure sands of the river Sulk . . . ," or describing whatever other commodity the merchant had for sale.

On they went, from the frontier town of Yazdir to the inner cities of Zamora. Conan and Subotai kept up their tireless pace, walk, jog-trot for an hour, and walk again; but the pace seemed slow to the barbarian. With his longer legs, he could easily have left his bowlegged companion far behind. The little man, moreover, grumbled about having to walk like a mere peasant instead of riding like a proper Hyrkanian warrior. Whenever they passed horses grazing in a field, Subotai suggested stealing a couple; but Conan, who had never ridden any animal, turned the idea aside.

At length the travelers came to the capital—Shadizar, the city of thieves, the abode of rogues. Here dwelt, in comparative safety, all the outlaws of the western world, even escaped slaves, exiles, and men with a price on their heads; for here they could safely hide, if they had the price should they be caught, and knew their ways around.

Conan found himself in the midst of a colorful throng. He rubbed shoulders with merchants in rich robes; artisans hawking trays of brass ornaments, gems, and weapons; bearded farmers in rough homespun, guiding to market wains laden with sacks of wheat and barley, sides of beef, and trussed, grunting pigs; stiff-backed soldiers, mobile-hipped whores, beggars, urchins, and priests. He saw squat Shemites with curly beards, lean Zuagirs in head cloths, kilted Brythunians, booted Corinthians, and turbaned Turanians.

Conan was amazed. Shadizar as far surpassed Yazdir in size and variety as Yazdir surpassed the towns of his Pit-fighting days. Never had he seen such a bewildering array of folk. It seemed to the Cimmerian that here was gathered a sampling of all the divers peoples of the earth.

Nor had he seen anything to equal the city's broad boulevards, pillared temples, domed palaces and mansions, and lush, walled gardens. He marveled that so many could dwell crowded together thus, without turning on one another to rend and slay, like savage beasts.

Not all sections of the city were so beautiful as the estates of the great lords and princes, with their marble columns and glimpses of parks and gardens. In the back streets he discovered crooked alleys swarming with hags and pimps, with painted children for sale to degenerates, with the poor and the ill. Here flesh was for sale, or at least for rent. Every pleasure, however decadent, could be had for money.

In these back streets lurked violence and sudden death, as well. Once, as Conan and Subotai strode through the crowd, a woman screamed. Men, cursing, scuttled away on furtive feet. In a trice, the two found themselves alone in the narrow way, with their hands on the hilts of their blades. At their feet, a man writhed as he clutched a wound in his belly from which a steady stream of blood trickled through his fingers.

"What . . ." began Conan uncertainly.

"Ask not," whispered Subotai. "Let us be gone, before the Watch comes by."

Conan shrugged as the Hyrkanian led him away by an obscure aperture between two buildings.

The narrow passageway opened into a broad, paved boulevard, lined with fashionable shops and stately trees. A procession occupied the center of the avenue; and the two strangers lingered to watch its passing.

The procession was led by a group of girls and young women, some scarcely more than children, who danced and chanted to the rhythm of myriads of tambourines. All were draped in soiled white garments, and garlands of wilted flowers crowned heads of unbound hair. Behind them marched ranks of youths beating time on deep-voiced drums, or making discordant music with cymbals, lyres, and plaintive flutes.

The eyes of all were glazed, unaware of the scene about them, like dreamers walking in their sleep. Among them stalked robed men with shaven pates, bearing brazen pots in which incense smoldered, to fill the air with seductive sweetness.

Conan wrinkled his nose at the sickly-sweet perfume of the vapors. The bizarre music was repugnant to him, and the strange behavior of the marchers alerted his keen barbarian senses to the presence of a nameless evil.

The dissonant music swelled as a band of naked youths came into view. Each had a serpent wound around his neck or shoulders or looped in thick coils about his arms. Each marched in total isolation from his fellows, as if he trod the soil of a separate world. Sunlight glinted on the polished scales of the reptiles, solid gray, or brown, or black, or, in some cases, splashed with mottled blotches or patterned in bright rings or diamonds.

"Are those things venomous?" Conan asked his companion.

"Some are. That brown one yonder is, if I mistake it not, a deadly cobra from Vendhya. And those big fellows, thicker than your arm, come from tropical jungles, many moons' journey to the south. They bear no poison; but if frightened or annoyed, they can loop a coil around a strong man's neck and strangle him to death."

"Ugh!" muttered Conan. The snakes revolted him, reminding him obscurely of the destruction of his Cimmerian home. Frowning, he turned to speak to Subotai but found him absorbed in staring at a young girl in the next group of marchers. The maiden, Conan saw, was a fragile beauty, despite her limp and dirty hair, her crown of withered flowers, and wide eyes lost in dreams. The flimsy shift she wore was torn and, with every step, exposed her naked thigh.

Eyeing the maiden hungrily, the thief shook his head. "Such a waste! A body like that should warm a warrior's bed o' nights, instead of being the plaything of priests and slithering serpents."

"What do you mean?" said Conan.

Subotai glanced at his large companion and saw that he did not jest. "Why, that wench, like all the rest, has given herself to the cult of Set, the Serpent. I hate all snakes and most priests, but above all I despise the worshipers of Set."

"A serpent god!" said Conan. "Would this have aught to do with the symbol that I seek?"

Subotai spread his upturned palms. Just then a shower of petals pelted the pair, and a laughing band of girls accosted them. These, bright-eyed and smiling, seemed less entranced than the maidens who were part of the procession.

"Come with us!" crooned one to Subotai.

"Not I, lass," said the Hyrkanian, a trifle wistfully. "I care not for snakes or the snake god."

"There is love in the arms of the serpent god such as men have never known," she murmured, swaying languorously. "Love that men can share. . . ."

Subotai snorted. "Since when have serpents had arms?"

As the girl walked off to try her blandishments on a more responsive onlooker, another girl glided up to Conan and tapped on his arm.

"Paradise awaits you, warrior," she whispered. "You need but follow me. . . ."

"Follow you whither?" growled Conan, sorely tempted to comply.

A merchant, standing at the doorway of his shop, stepped forward. "Stranger, beware," he said in a low tone to the Cimmerian. "The servants of Set are deceivers. They worship Death."

"Do they indeed?" Conan was shocked. To him, Death was ever the enemy.

The merchant nodded. "They would murder their own parents, thinking to confer a boon by relieving them of the burden of life."

Conan nodded curt thanks and watched the girl melt into the crowd.

A shadow passed between the sun and the young Cimmerian. Conan looked up to see a sumptuous palanquin borne on the shoulders of eight young women. Draped in embroidered silk of regal purple tied back with ropes of gold, the chair itself was a thing of opulence; but it was not for this marvel that Conan's eyes widened in astonishment and he drew in a sudden breath. For riding in the princely litter sat a creature of such beauty as he had never imagined.

As the risen sun makes pale the lingering moon, so this woman outshone all women he had ever seen and turned them to inconsequential ghosts.

A cascade of sable hair fell to her waist; sapphire eyes sparkled in the sculptured oval of her face; her full lips were as moist as morning dew. Her figure, lithe and strong, was clad in the gold-encrusted garment of a priestess; and when she moved to acknowledge the cheering throng, her robe parted to reveal a pale, exquisite thigh.

Reading the look in Conan's awe-struck eyes, Subotai hissed, "Don't stare like that! She is a royal princess."

As if ensorcelled, the barbarian remained transfixed. It was as if he had not heard the warning. And at that moment, the priestess's gaze fell upon Conan. A light flashed in her gem-bright eyes, and her lips parted for a sudden breath. With an upraised hand, she stayed the swaying progress of her litter.

"You, warrior!" called the princess in a soft, husky voice whose reverberations stirred the Cimmerian's blood.

"Yes, my lady?"

The woman's voice enveloped the youth as a breaking wave constrains a swimmer in the surging sea. "Throw away your sword and come with us. Eschew the red trail of war. Return to the simple life—to the eternal cycle of the seasons.

"A cleansing time already waits at the edge of the world, a time of renewal after the downfall of all things old and decadent. Join us and you shall be renewed as are the serpents of the grass, who shed their outgrown skins and live again, young and swift, agile and beautiful."

Conan shook his tousled head to clear it of the eddying incense, the better to grasp the meaning of the cryptic words uttered so fervently. But the woman read his gesture as a refusal; for when he looked up again, she had drawn the curtains of her palanquin, and was being borne away by her handmaidens.

Conan stared bemused. Never had any woman seemed so desirable. When Subotai plucked at his sleeve, Conan shook him off and started to follow the vanishing litter. Alarmed, the small man scampered after him.

Presently, the avenue opened out into a large, tree-lined square where the caravans gathered. Here was a miniature city, a teeming town of camel's hair tents and gaily-colored yurts of beaten felt. Lines of asses, mules, and camels were tethered in the center of the square, amid the abodes of their owners; while all around the edges rose the protective walls of the caravanserais, wherein weary travelers could seek food and rest.

Beyond this busy crossroads gathering place, Conan saw a slender dark tower piercing the tenuous fabric of the sky. Despite the brilliance of the day, the tower seemed draped in shadows. Toward this grim pinnacle, Conan saw the procession wend its way; shouldering passersby aside, he sought to overtake the litter and its beautiful occupant.

The distance had dwindled to a few short strides, when Conan froze in his tracks. As those in the lead of the procession prepared to enter the gaping doorway to the tower, a chant arose and floated back above the noises of the street.

"Doom . . . Doom . . . Doom . . ."

Confusion, fear, and a surge of anger contorted the face of the young Cimmerian as that ominous chant awoke images long dormant in his memory. So bitter were the feelings welling up in his heart that he scarcely saw the final groups of marchers, who passed an arm's length from him. These were young men, scarcely more than boys, who staggered along, faces blank and drained of color, lashing their naked flesh. The whips with which they beat their backs and shoulders were made of the hides of serpents and barbed with snakes' fangs, cleverly inserted, so that with each stroke the flagellants' flesh was beaded with their blood. Seemingly unaware of pain, they chanted as they went. "Doom . . . Doom . . . Thulsa Doom . . . Thulsa Doom. . . ."

Conan watched grimly until the last of the procession entered into the forbidding tower. "In Shadizar, in Zamora," the witch had said, "you will find that which you seek." And already he had found the fanatic worshipers of a man or god or devil who bore the name of Doom.

"Fools!" snapped Subotai, spitting on the pavement. "Fools and madmen, snake-lovers, death-worshipers! Everywhere in these lands they rear those dark towers, the citadels of Set. Always it is the same: they lure the young and innocent into their toils—innocents who forsake husbands, sweethearts, and family to make love with serpents and mad priests, in orgies of foulness."

"Who was the woman you called a royal princess?" demanded Conan. "Isn't she a priestess of the snake cult?" He remembered with a mingling of loathing and desire the serpents, embroidered in gold and silver thread, that writhed across her robe.

"That woman, as you call her," said Subotai, "is the Princess Yasimina, daughter of King Osric and heir to the Ruby Throne. You must have seen the royal sigil on her pendant—you were staring openly enough!"

"What would a king's daughter be doing amongst those snake-besotted votaries?"

Subotai grimaced. "She's one of them, a high priestess of Set. Long ago the priests entrapped her with their lies and drugs. They are deceivers, all, as the merchant told. 'Tis whispered that they fall in with strangers on the road to strangle them as they sleep or to stab them in the dark—all for the honor of their slithering god. Death lurks behind those dreamy eyes, barbarian."

"Does King Osric foster this strange religion? Is he also one of them?"

"Nay. He much bemoans the fate of his only child."

"Then, if the snake-worshipers displease him, why doesn't he send soldiers out to round them up and slay them?"

"The priests are powerful men," explained the Hyrkanian. "Osric dares not move against them openly, for many in Zamora deem him a foreigner and no proper king. His sire was a Corinthian adventurer who rose to generalship in the Zamorian army and seized the throne to which the son clings by a fingernail. But why this sudden interest in the fading fortunes of a weakling? His fate means nothing to the likes of us."

"These are strange lands," mumbled Conan, "and those who dwell here are stranger still."

VI

The Thief

The two adventurers explored the winding ways of Shadizar, for want of other entertainment. They strolled through broad streets and mean alleys at random, drinking in the sights and sounds and smells so new to the barbarian. And as they went, Conan pondered his quest. He assumed, perhaps wrongly, that the witch in the hillside house had directed him here for some reason. So far, beyond the chanting of the word "Doom," he had found nothing to remind him of the Vanir raiders or their leader's sinister standard—nothing save a cult of snake-worshipers devoted to an evil god. The serpentine element in both might be a mere coincidence.

The sun, like an orange-red ball, dropped behind the jagged roofs of tall buildings and the sharp point of the lowering tower. Lights came on in the tents in the big square. Dogs slunk through the shadows, seeking garbage; furtive faces with predatory eyes leered from dark doorways on latticed windows; and, as the traffic dwindled, bonfires blazed in the streets where beggars converged for warmth and companionship.

Finding a food stall, the sightseers squandered on a good meal some of the silver filched from the dead soldier.

Conan munched a slab of roast pig, while his companion questioned the proprietor.

"I am a Kerlait," the Hyrkanian said conversationally. "The ensign of my clan has always been nine yak tails and a horse's skull. Have you chanced to see a standard such as that?"

The shopkeeper, looking bored, claimed ignorance, but mentioned that he had heard travelers speak of such a thing.

"Standards are a matter of interest to me," confided Subotai genially. "Perhaps I should have been a herald!" After a pause, he added with a disarming grin, "I came on one you may have seen—two black snakes face to face, upholding a black sun with their knotted tails . . ."

Subotai's voice trailed off on a questioning note. The food-vendor yawned indifferently.

"I seldom notice such things; they do not intrigue me. The only snakes hereabouts are those of Set, worshiped in accursed towers like that one yonder."

Conan asked sharply, "Are there other towers, then?"

The vendor nodded. "There are many throughout Zamora. At least one in every town or city, so I've heard. All recent masonry, you will understand, stranger; for only in the past few years has the Set cult spread so wide."

"Oh," said Conan. His interest spurred the shopkeeper to vouchsafe a further confidence.

"Not long ago, the Set cult was but a little band; now they are everywhere."

"Is it so?" marveled Subotai, with a knowing wink at the young Cimmerian by his side.

"Aye! But yonder spire is the mother of them all. 'The Tower of the Black Serpent' they call it, and so it is known near and far. . . ."

A glint of amusement flared in the Hyrkanian's eyes. He opened his mouth to ask another question; but Conan forestalled him.

"The marchers this afternoon were chanting a name, something like 'Doom.' Know you if this is the name of a man?"

The vendor shrugged. "I leave them alone, so they will leave me alone. I know nothing about their order. Some say they are murderers, loving death more than life, and the embraces of their venomous serpents more than the embrace of human arms. But I say naught against them. . . . Look you, young sirs, something I had from an Easterling merchant only this morn."

He displayed a silk pouch filled with withered petals of an ebon hue. "Black Lotus, from Khitai," he whispered. "The very best!"

Subotai licked his lips. Silver changed hands; and, when they strolled away, the small man clutched the pouch. He slipped one of the petals under his tongue, and offered one to Conan. The Cimmerian shook his head.

In the following days, Conan tried to find work as a guard or a soldier, but those to whom he applied dismissed his stumbling requests, put off by his few broken words of Zamorian. At length, after buying another meal for the two of them, Conan told Subotai, "There goes the last of our money. We have paid our lodging for tonight, but what shall we do for tomorrow?"

Sitting at the table in the cookshop that had taken the last of their coppers, Subotai pondered. "You could sell that pendant hanging about your neck. It is a strange device, and finely crafted."

"I found this in the witch's hut," objected the barbarian, "and I doubt not that it serves to ward off evil. Besides, it is a rich man's toy; it will be thought I stole it."

"Beggars cannot chose," shrugged the Hyrkanian. "Unless you wish to sell your ancient sword. It, too, would fetch a handsome price."

"The sword, never!" exclaimed Conan. "It saved me from the wolves. It will serve me well in times to come. It is such a weapon as my father might have made."

"Then we starve tomorrow." The small man shrugged. "I am more used to that than you, Cimmerian."

"If you hadn't spent so much on that accursed Black Lotus stuff, we should still have the means for food and lodging!"

Subotai choked back an angry reply and finished his repast in silence. The two were fast becoming friends, and neither relished the thought of parting over such a quarrel.

At length, Conan rumbled, "Take me to a jewel seller who buys craft from distant places."

Subotai, grinning behind a sheltering hand, led the Cimmerian to the thieves' quarter, known as the Maul. As they passed the Tower of Set, the infamous Stygian serpent god, Conan stared at its majestic height.

"You know what's in there, well guarded by the votaries?" asked Subotai with a sly look at his companion.

"No."

"Jewels . . . riches without end. And the greatest jewel of all, called the Eye of the Serpent . . . it's supposed to have powers beyond a man's imagining. . . . And do you know what else is there?"

"No."

"Snakes. It is the home of all those serpents you saw in the procession. Do you want to have a snake, like the worshipers of Set?"

"Enough. We have our work cut out for us," snapped Conan. But his eyes, the eyes of a mountain-bred man, scaled off the edifice judging it as he would a rock wall in the homeland of Cimmeria. Yes, it might be breached . . . if one had the right equipment, courage, and a sturdy sword.

Subotai led his friend down several back alleys. Along one, a hag, bent and grizzled, beckoned to them with some strange religious artifact.

"A pittance, to protect you from evil," she begged.

"I have need of that pittance as much as you, old woman," said Subotai. "I am evil!" He laughed.

"May the milk of your mother turn sour!" she spat as she hobbled off.

As the two companions threaded their way through the street of the whores, filthy wenches sidled up to them.

"Here are the gates of heaven," one wheedled, smiling at Conan as she lifted her garment to display a shapely thigh.

"Too bad we have no money for a fee," said Subotai. "I fear they would not love us for ourselves." Remembering the night in the demon-witch's house, Conan looked at the Hyrkanian with faint disgust.

On the street of the animals, Conan's feeling of disgust

became abhorrence. All around them, they encountered beasts of every species, many from lands unknown to the Cimmerian. They grunted, snarled, barked, and bleated; and the ground was sodden with their excrement. Traders argued and whined over prices, so intently that they scarcely marked the passage of the strangers.

"Does it always smell like this?" Conan asked. "How does a cleansing wind come in to blow the stench away?"

Subotai said nothing; for there was no answer to the hillman's question.

Moments later, Conan glanced into the open door of a shabby shop. He glimpsed a bizarre ritual in progress, one he could not comprehend, save that it involved several naked boys and a pure white cow.

"Is there no end to the obscenities committed in the name of civilization?" he asked Subotai.

"Not in Shadizar, at least," said the Hyrkanian with the unconcern born of long experience. Conan stared in silence at a deformed thing that scurried away before him. He felt the freak was a symbol of all the evil man had wrought when he built large habitations for humanity.

The Maul was the lurking place of rapists, murderers, and perverts. Here, too, congregated thieves and those who sold the goods they stole to merchants who were less squeamish than their fellows.

The companions found the stall of a merchant of gems —an ill-kept place, which could quickly be abandoned if the constabulary should come seeking the proprietor. Conan slipped the jewel-set sigil from his burly neck and handed it to the man, an elderly Shemite, judging by his turban and gray, curling beard. The sharp-eyed fellow appraised the seller—or so it seemed—far more closely than the object to be sold.

"This is old, very old," he muttered, after examining the pendant with cursory interest. "It comes from some exotic land, eastward a thousand leagues or more. It shows the wear of centuries."

"What mean the symbols carved between the rubies that encrust the strange design?" asked Conan. "They speak of magic—or so it seems to me."

The Shemite shot a searching glance at the young

Cimmerian. Although avarice gleamed in his beady eyes, his answer came with studied indifference.

"The thing is ancient and much worn. Not too much value there," he said. "As for magic, who knows which things have magic, unless such properties can be shown? I'll give you two crowns five, and that's a generous offer." He turned his back and started to dust a shelf of merchandise.

"Done," said Conan quickly, ignoring the light tug on his sleeve.

The man swung back and dropped the small gold pieces into Conan's outstretched palm. As the friends walked away, Subotai exploded.

"Fool! Ninny! Any idiot knows you never take the first offer. I could have got you twice or thrice the price with a little haggling."

Conan scowled at his companion. "Why didn't you say so at the time?"

"You did not say what you proposed to do, and one does not jostle the archer's arm when he has drawn the shaft."

The turbulence of Conan's anger quickly faded to a sigh. He said, "I fear me you have the right of it. I have never learned the customs of the marketplace. The next time we must chaffer, I'll give the task to you."

"Admission of ignorance," said the Hyrkanian, "is the beginning of wisdom, as some Khitaian philosopher liked to say. Don't look so downcast; we have enough for a fortnight's worth of food. Before that, something will turn up, I'm sure."

Conan grunted. "And if it does not, what shall we do then? I must find the bearer of that emblem and him who slew my parents—my Cimmerian honor demands it!"

"To the Nine Hells with your snaky emblem and your Cimmerian vengeance!" Subotai nodded toward the dark tower, which, silent and forbidding, could be seen from every street and alley. "I think I have a plan to make us rich as lords. . . ."

"You have more plans than an ass has feet," growled Conan. "What is this plan of yours?"

"If this is indeed the Tower of the Black Serpent, as

our informant named it, then I have heard of it betimes . . . in a professional way, you understand, from my brother thieves."

"Heard what?"

"That it contains fabulous riches," whispered Subotai, licking dry lips. "Thither comes the tribute of the believers from every Set cult in the kingdom—gold, drugs, jewels, wine, and women! But in particular come jewels. The Set worshipers prize polished precious stones, deep and unwinking like the eyes of the serpents they adore."

Conan grunted. He had never in his life stolen anything more than a piece of fruit from the tree of a Cimmerian neighbor, unless one counted the looting of the dead Hyrkanian and the vanished witch's cave. And until he had met Subotai, he had despised all thieves. Cimmerian villagers did not steal from one another, although they freely raided the lands of clans with whom they were at feud.

Now, in a city, with his money low and his chances of employment poor until he could better master the language of Zamora, he knew he must find some means of satisfying his leonine appetite. Seeing his hesitation, Subotai continued.

"They say the tower harbors the greatest jewel of all. The 'Eye of the Serpent,' 'tis called—a gem of such rarity that we could buy a dukedom with it. It's said to have mystic powers, too; but I heed not such rumors. Its value in hard money is enough."

Conan continued skeptical. "Such a treasure, without doubt, is guarded well."

"Aye," Subotai nodded wisely, "but not by men! 'Tis said by serpents, which roam freely about the tower and its winding ways, as dogs do wander about the yurts of my people."

"So?" said Conan.

Subotai spread greasy palms. "You look for snakes; I look for treasure. Mayhap we could find them both in yonder spire. . . ."

In the end it was agreed to break into the tower, although the Cimmerian little liked the idea. The next day, hunched over a frugal dinner, they outlined a plan, their conspiratorial whispers masked by the crackling of a hot fire on a stone hearth. Recklessly, they decided to embark on the venture that very night, since the overcast skies would shroud the full moon, making it a perfect occasion for a burglary.

Gloom wrapped the two in a velvet cloak of darkness as they crept along the shoulder of a craggy rise from whose crest the dark tower soared into the clouded heavens. A wall, hung with leafy vines, as with some ancient tapestry, guarded the base of the knoll. No rope ladder could have provided them with easier access to the temple precincts than those sturdy, interwoven vines. Subotai scuttled over the wall first, being the lighter of the two; and once over, he signaled his success with a low bird-call. The young Cimmerian made his ascent.

Concealed behind a blanket of low shrubs, the thieves studied the slope between them and the tower's base. Gnarled trees raised threatening branches, as if to warn them off. Sharp-toothed rocks thrust up their pointed fangs through the infertile soil. The tower, black against the shrouded skies, soared upward, a cylinder of sleek, dark stone tapering to a lofty peak. And between the tower and the sheltering shrubs, a reflecting pool stretched its gaping mouth in a soundless shriek. The intruders were about to leave their hiding place and approach the tower when a twig snapped underfoot and a shape materialized from the deeper shadows of the curved tower wall.

Just then an icicle of silver moonlight speared through a rift in the cloudy vapors, to reveal the form of the newcomer. It was a woman, young and beautiful. Moonfire cascaded over her slender shoulders, and played on one bare, muscular thigh and the long, slender leg of a dancer or acrobat. Conan held his breath, for the woman was superbly desirable from what he could see of her.

Over tight undergarments of black silk, she wore an abbreviated suit of black leather, which left her arms and legs bare; and in that momentary shaft of white moonlight, Conan saw that the woman's limbs were sun-bronzed and endowed with steely strength. Her buskins were tight-laced about her feet, and the blonde hair, rippling about her leather-clad shoulders, was bound out of her way by rings of ebony. A band of metal, somber in hue, protected her brow; while slung from her girdle were a knotted length of silken cord and a three-pronged grappling hook. A curved knife, almost as long as a saber, was strapped in its sheath against her thigh.

Conan shifted his weight, and a dry leaf rustled beneath him. The woman darted a glance in his direction, and the curved blade hissed from its sheath to point at Conan's chest, as if the woman's eyes could penetrate the darkness like the eyes of a cat. Since further concealment was useless, Conan slowly rose to his feet, keeping both hands in plain sight. The balance and shaping of the sword, he saw, made it as useful for throwing as for thrusting.

Conan and the woman looked at each other for a wordless moment, as the shaft of light diminished and died. "You are no guard," murmured Conan.

"No more are you," the girl retorted. "And who is that beside you who tries to make no sound but breathes as heavily as a fat man?"

"Another thief," replied Subotai, rising to his feet. "I fear it is one whose skills are a little rusty."

"And who and whence are you?" The girl addressed Conan coolly.

"I am Conan, a Cimmerian, a manslayer by profession, a thief from necessity. This is Subotai, the Hyrkanian . . ."

"A thief both by choice and profession," said his comrade with a touch of pride. "We come to plunder the snake-lovers of their riches."

The girl smiled broadly, her white teeth visible despite the shadows. "You are two fools who laugh at certain death! You do not even have a rope and tackle. How, then, do you plan to ascend the tower—fly on the back of a dragon? There are no windows on the lower floors."

"I have my means," said Subotai, "though my friend is less prepared. And who, good wench, are you?"

"I am Valeria," she answered shortly.

Subotai gasped. "Not *the* Valeria?"

As the girl nodded, Conan shot a puzzled glance at his companion.

"This is a famous lady, Conan. A very queen of thieves, they say. But tell me, lady, where is your band of brigands? You could not mean to dare the serpent's tower alone."

The girl shrugged. "They're fools and cowards all! Some scared of snakebite; others afraid of the demon Set; all dreading the man called Doom."

Conan started at the mention of that name; and sharp-eyed Valeria noticed the tensing of his massive frame.

"You do not fear that name, Cimmerian. But it means something to you, I do think. Those in the tower worship strange gods; are you among them?"

"They are not my gods, girl," growled Conan.

She shrugged and turned her attention to the tower. "Horrors lurk behind those dark walls," she murmured.

"And wealth as well," said Subotai.

Valeria smiled. "Then you shall go first, little man."

In the end it was Conan who first climbed the Tower of the Black Serpent. It took three throws of the grapnel to lodge it securely in the masonry at the tower's upper rim. Conan tried the slender silken rope and found that it held his weight. Subotai ignored these preparations; he was occupied hooking talonlike steel spikes to his footwear and binding a pair of bronzen hooks about his wrists and lower arms. Then he sank the blades into the mortar between the smooth stones and grinned.

"I do not trust myself to ropes," he said. "I will climb my own way."

"Suit yourself," said Conan with a shrug.

"Less talk," snapped Valeria. "The wealth of half the world is at our fingertips, and you waste time in useless chatter."

With a grunt, Conan began the ascent. Valeria clambered after him, her slender body moving up the wall with effortless agility. Laughing, she looked over her shoulder at the laboring Hyrkanian and asked, "Do you want to live forever?"

"I'm coming as fast as I can," panted Subotai, his quiver and bow case bulking like a hump on his back. And muttering to himself, he added, "This woman climbs like a cat, and spits like one, too."

Below the climbers, the darkness deepened, but they seldom looked down. Above, the cloud cover was breaking, as fresh winds awoke in the East. The moon glared down at them with its great white eye, as if to expose them for all the world to see. Conan cursed and glanced at the sleeping city stretched below, wearing its lights from bonfire and hearth like a necklace of topaz, gold, and luminescent pearls. He was as high above the empty thoroughfares as any sentinel pacing the towers of the nearby royal palace. The thought made him uneasy, and he quickened his pace.

Soon he came upon a narrow window, whence shone a pulsating light. Within he heard strange, discordant music and a muffled drumbeat. There came to his ears a faint chorus of hissing voices that did not sound like human whisperings, as sickly-sweet incense made its way to his nostrils. Suddenly, an enormous head reared up in the embrasure. Cold, slit-pupiled eyes stared into Conan's, while a forked tongue flickered out to taste the air. Conan started back, almost losing his grip upon the rope, until he perceived that a pane of glass separated him from the giant reptile.

Resuming his climb, Conan reached the parapet. Here the merlons rose from the rim like the points of a crown, and embedded in the mortar were myriads of bright-hued gems that glimmered like frost under the moon's magnificence and, in the shifting rays, fractured into a thousand tiny rainbows.

With a sigh, Conan levered himself over the parapet; but as he dropped to the walkway inside the battlement, a huge figure, roughly human in shape but with an apelike length of arm, rushed upon him. The creature—man, demon, or ape, Conan knew not which—dealt him an unexpected blow that hurled him to the pavement.

As the Cimmerian rolled to his feet and snatched out his dagger, he saw that, while his adversary was wrapped in a hooded cloak, its exposed hands were covered with glittering scales. Instead of preparing to finish the intruder off, the creature was bent over the embrasure, fumbling at the grapnel hooks to cast down the rope to which Valeria mutely clung.

Conan sprang on the back of the thing and stabbed repeatedly. The torn fabric parted to reveal a fungoid growth protruding from the base of its neck, between its thick-muscled shoulders. Directly, the puffy growth parted, and a red eye glared forth. In a spasm of horror, Conan struck, extinguishing the orb. Liquid, spurting from the wound, splashed on the barbarian's chest. As he withdrew his weapon to strike again, the creature whirled about, and huge, scaly hands locked on Conan's throat.

Conan slammed the obscene head against the parapet and sank his dagger into the monster's belly. Coughing blood, the creature sagged against the battlements, releasing its stranglehold. As he fought for breath, the Cimmerian beheld a being from the depths of a nightmare. Blind eyes, dripping mucus, rolled in deep pits; a wide, lipless gash of mouth yawned, froglike, from folds of leprous skin. Crouching like a springing leopard, Conan grasped the inert form and, using all his fighting skills, rose to full height to fling it over the jewel-encrusted parapet. A diminishing wail drifted skyward, followed by a soggy thump.

Close behind him, a woman laughed. As he whirled, Conan saw that Valeria had drawn herself through an embrasure and now leaned with negligent grace against a parapet.

"For a thief, you make a good killer," she chuckled.

"For a thief, you climb like a mountain man," he replied, wiping his dagger and sheathing it.

VII

The Gem

"Hoy!" came a hoarse whisper from below the tower's rim. Conan and Valeria turned to see Subotai, breathing hard as he levered himself up the tower wall.

"I see you've been busy," grunted the Hyrkanian when they had helped him through the embrasure. "What was that tumbling thing that nearly knocked me from my spikes?"

"Crom knows," muttered Conan. "Some hell-spawn fetched hither by the priests. Are you all right?"

"Aye, given a moment to catch my breath."

Valeria ran her hands over the jewels incrusted in the battlements. "A fortune here!" she breathed. "And ours for the taking!"

Sliding her dagger from its sheath, Valeria tried to pry a large sapphire from its enshrouding mortar. Subotai drew his unstrung bow from its case, placed one end on the rough-hewn pave, and strung it. Then he studied Valeria.

"Leave off picking at those pretty pebbles, my lady," he said. "They're worth a pittance compared to what lies below. Besides, you'll dull your blade, and you may need it soon."

"Let's move," growled Conan, "before some priest or guard stumbles on us."

Valeria poured her handful of loosened gems into her

belt-wallet. "To work, then," she said, striding to the
narrow door that broke the circular line of the roof tiles. She
grasped the carved handle and pulled vigorously in expecta-
tion of resistance; but the door swung back so easily that it
almost overbalanced the girl. Peering through the open
doorway, Conan frowned at the dim green glow within but
Valeria, walking lithely on the balls of her feet, marched
boldly in. Conan followed closely. He had an impression of
a floor half-concealed by knee-high swirls of mist, a circle
of stone columns supporting the roof, and a frieze along the
walls between the columns. A soul-chilling, eerie light,
reflected by the tenuous layer of mist, obscured further
details.

As the mist, released from the confines of the small
rotunda, dispersed through the open door, Conan perceived
a circular, well-like opening in the center of the floor-
boards, from the depths of which emanated an emerald
glow and the muffled sound of rhythmic chanting. Borne on
the mists, a putrid odor wafted up. Valeria thrust a hand
across her face; Subotai wrinkled his nose.

"What plant or animal could stink like that?" he
whispered.

"A three-day-old battlefield," Conan rumbled. "That's
carrion, or I'm a Hyrkanian."

"Look at this!" breathed Valeria. She pointed to the
rim of the well, whence descended a series of iron rungs,
forming a narrow ladder. Nearby an enormous hook protruded; and on it hung a pulley. Through this pulley a stout
rope was threaded, the ends of which fell away into
obscurity.

Conan studied the contraption. "The beast-thing I
killed probably ascended the iron ladder. But if there was
need for haste, it might have ridden upward on this rope
—assuming there be some counterweight below. We'll use
the rungs, knowing nought of that."

"I'd trust my own rope more," whispered Valeria,
frowning. "Those rungs look far apart and ill-fixed to the
well wall."

"Come on, girl!" muttered Conan, lowering himself
over the edge of the narrow platform. "If the rungs could
bear the beast-thing, they'll support our weight."

Masking her fear in a proud display of courage, Valeria swung out into the void, sought out a rung with a wary toe, and began the descent. Subotai, clutching his strung bow and a single arrow in one fist, came last.

In silence they made their way into the unknown depths. Polished stones of a darkling hue, set with bright gems, made mockery of the star-tossed firmament beyond the tower's pinnacle; for in the confines of the well, it seemed the very skies pressed in upon them with ominous intent. As each uncertain step was taken, the distant chanting swelled in volume, and the carrion stench enveloped them.

At last they felt a cut-stone floor beneath their feet and saw the source of the almondine illumination. They stood in a round rock chamber, from which two darkened openings led away. A third aperture, the size of a large door, was blocked by an iron grating of widely-spaced bars; and it was through these bars that the strange light pushed its demoniac way. To Conan's astonishment, near where they stood, another well-throat gaped into utter darkness.

Through the bars, Conan and his companions, approaching carefully, could see a huge, pillared hall, lit by a pulsing emerald light. The floor of that great chamber glowed in the strange luminescence like the unbroken surface of a silent pond. Valeria whispered, "How could they fit this hall into the tower? It's far too big!"

"We must have descended far below the level of the street," muttered Conan.

He and Valeria exchanged a glance, an opulent design of curiosity stitched by needles of fear. Then the girl shrugged and slid her slender body between the bars of the grating. Conan followed with more difficult; he had to turn sidewise and exhale sharply to force his massive shoulders through. Subotai, lithe as an eel despite his armaments, joined them.

Beyond the shadows in which they paused, between two rows of columns, a group of robed figures stood with their backs to the intruders. At the farthest end of the rock-hewn hall, another man occupied some sort of ledge or balcony, his body clearly visible above the heads of the massed and reverent throng. In the bright light that was focused on him, Conan saw that he was a man of gigantic size, and black of skin. A magnificent specimen of virile manhood, the black stood, half naked, hands raised and eyes closed, intoning the sonorous chant which had broken the silence.

Valeria nudged Conan. "That is Yaro, second in the hierachy," she whispered. "Only the man called Doom stands higher in the cult."

For a moment, Conan was riveted to the spot at the mention of that name; but he said nothing. Subotai murmured: "I have heard of such black men from countries far to the south. Is this Yaro, then, a Kushite?"

Valeria shrugged. "They say he is a thousand years old; so Bel and Ishtar alone know whence he hails."

"Our way is blocked with worshipers," said Conan softly. "How shall we pass them without raising an alarm?"

"Let's work our way around the side," whispered Valeria. "I think there is another, lower level, and without doubt a stair to reach it by."

She glided from pillar to pillar, a silent shadow among the shadows, followed by Conan and Subotai. When they had almost reached the area in which stood the congregation, Valeria pointed to a dungeon-black stairwell. "You two go down," she breathed, "to see what's there. I'll stay here for the time to guard your back."

The two men, tense with apprehension, descended a narrow, winding stair amid motionless, fetid air, which bore to their nostrils an ever-waxing stench. At length they reached another vaulted chamber, lit but feebly through a round opening in the ceiling. This aperture, Conan realized, connected the room in which they stood with that in which the ceremony they had glimpsed was in progress.

As they felt their way through the foul air, Subotai started and hissed, "Erlik's blood, Conan! Look at that!"

The floor beneath the circular opening was littered with corpses, male and female. Some appeared fresh; others were far gone in decay; still others had been reduced to skeletal remains. As the men edged closer to the mass of putrescence, rats fled squeaking before them, their eyes aglow with hostility when, upon reaching safety, the rodents turned briefly to watch the intruders.

Veiled in the darkness beyond the opening, Conan looked up. He could see Yaro kneeling on his balcony. As the black man rose, the chanting faded to a whisper. Moving as silently as a stalking panther, the Cimmerian skirted the shamble of corpses and positioned himself directly below the leader, whence, unseen, he could observe the faces of the foremost rank of worshipers. The cultists seemed to be young persons of both sexes, although their hoods shadowed their rapt faces and their long robes hid their bodies.

As Conan watched, one of the group stepped forward, discarding its hooded robe. Revealed in the emerald light was a beautiful young woman, whose slender body was scarcely shielded by a gauzy wisp of fabric. With resolute step, the maiden mounted a stone corbel that jutted out like a spar from the side of the aperture; and as she moved, the solemn chanting swelled in volume.

Subotai plucked at Conan's sleeve and pointed to a low archway at the far side of the chamber. Conan tore his gaze away from the girl poised above the pit, and followed the Hyrkanian. Scrambling to get through the waist-high opening, Conan found himself in a rotunda some twenty paces across, with no entry or egress save that through which they had come. A pair of lamps, supported by ornate wall brackets, cast a fitful light across the curvate walls.

The center of the room was occupied by a truncated stone pylon or altar, awrithe with carved figures and glyphs. "The Eye of the Serpent!" hissed Subotai, pointing. "Gods, look at that!"

Conan's glance, obedient to the Hyrkanian's eager gesture, revealed an enormous ruby-red jewel of teardrop shape, resting upon the stone pylon. Then a slight movement drew his attention to the altar's base. Coiled about the stela was a serpent of prodigious size. No snake so large in girth had the young Cimmerian ever heard of, or even imagined. The lamplight in the chamber sparkled on the glittering scales that clothed the sinuous length of the monstrous reptile, and added immeasurably to its apparent magnitude.

"The rarest gem on earth, and the largest, by Mitra!"

panted Subotai. "We could buy an emirate in Turan with it."

"Aye, if we could lay hand on it. Do you see what guards it?"

Subotai inhaled a shocked breath, as he contemplated the enormity before them.

Conan took a cautious step forward. "Does it sleep or wake?" he whispered. "Its eyes are open."

"You can't tell with snakes," said Subotai. "They have no eyelids."

Conan took two more steps, but still the serpent remained motionless. "Could I but sever its neck with one mighty blow . . ." he muttered.

"Oh, no!" said Subotai. "You little comprehend how long it takes for such vermin to die. In its thrashings, the headless body would crush us to pulp."

"Well, then," growled Conan, "we must take the gem without arousing the brute. Here!"

Moving as softly as he could, Conan pulled his baldric over his head and handed his scabbarded weapon to the Hyrkanian. Then he glided toward the pylon and its scaly guardian. When only a hand's breadth separated his feet from the bulging coils of the creature, Conan stretched out his arm; but the ruby gem remained tantalizingly beyond his reach.

Conan drew back, frowning in thought. If he let his body topple forward, bracing his chest against the pylon, he could reach the jewel without touching the serpent's coils. If he failed, he would surely die. He drew a deep breath, stiffened his back, and, standing on his toes, fell forward, until his outstretched hands made contact with the altar's edge and broke his fall.

Tightening the grasp of his right hand, he stretched forth his left to pluck the gem from the indentation in the carven surface on which it lay. Although the jewel felt icy cold against his palm, Conan tucked the stone into his tunic. He was about to try to regain his balance when another object on the altar caught his eye.

Next to the hollow in which the gem had reposed lay a small bronze medallion, embossed with a design that, despite the dim light, awoke echoes in the barbarian's mind.

At the sight of two writhing serpents with intertwining tails, Conan's memory fled back to the dreadful day in his childhood when, through the snow-trampled rutted road of his Cimmerian village, wheeling horsemen drove their merciless dogs and raised their swords against defenseless villagers. And he remembered the glittering arc made by Doom's sword—his father's sword—and his mother's severed head. . . .

It was a grim-faced Conan who clamped the medallion between his jaws and heaved himself into an upright position. Turning, he started toward the low archway, when a look of horror crossed the Hyrkanian's face.

"Behind you!" croaked Subotai, his vocal chords half paralyzed with terror.

Conan whipped around to find that the serpent had awakened. The great wedge-shaped head, as large as that of a horse, rose to the height of a man. The slavering jaws opened, like a miniature drawbridge, to reveal rows of dagger fangs.

When the huge body lunged forward, Conan whipped out his long-bladed dirk; and as the snake's head approached, he struck with the tigerish speed of a trained killer. The dagger's needle point impaled the serpent's lower jaw and drove in through the reptile's palate, pinning the wicked jaws together.

Hissing, the wounded serpent threw a confining coil about its attacker's body, immobilizing one of Conan's arms. A jerk of the creature's head tore the dirk out of the barbarian's grasp and carried it out of reach. Struggling to tear loose the deadly coil, Conan staggered back against the wall of the chamber, but to no avail. The snake threw a second coil about him.

Conan's face blackened as the relentless coils squeezed the breath from his body. With his free arm, the Cimmerian sought to batter the serpentine head against the wall; but so large and powerful was the reptile that his effort was futile.

In an agony of fear, Subotai danced about trying to get a clear shot at the serpent without further endangering his friend. At last, he nocked an arrow and released his bowstring. The missile sank halfway into the scaly neck, but the serpent seemed to feel nothing. It whipped another murderous coil about the Cimmerian's legs, nearly dragging him to the ground.

With a mighty heave of chest and shoulders, Conan managed to force the serpent's head against the wall, so that the dagger point, which protruded from the creature's skull, scrapped on the mortar between two stones. With his remaining strength, the barbarian pounded the pommel of the dirk with his free fist, driving the point into the crumbling mortar.

During that momentary respite, Subotai shot another arrow; then a third. This missile drove through the serpent's neck and pierced the mortar, immobilizing the reptile. As it thrashed about to free itself, it loosed its grip on its adversary, and Conan reeling from the exertion, fought free.

"Catch, Conan, catch!" hissed Subotai, tossing the barbarian's sword to him, hilt first. Conan caught the weapon and wheeled, just as the snake pulled loose from its insecure restraint. As the scaly body plunged toward the Cimmerian, he raised the sword and, with two mighty hands upon the pommel, brought the blade down across the serpent's neck, severing the head.

"Watch out!" called Subotai, as the headless body thrashed like a giant whip, knocking Conan to the ground and sending the Hyrkanian flying across the empty altar. Slowly, the reptilian thrashings ceased as the creature's life-blood ebbed; and the battered adventurers gathered up their scattered gear and made their way back into the carrion-littered hall.

In the hall above, the ceremony neared its climax. Conan saw the black priest, Yaro, rise to his full height. At his commanding gesture, the mesmerized girl poised on the jutting corbel, raised her arms, and fell or threw herself into the corpse-filled pit.

A chorus of cries of surprise and superstitious terror filled the darkened chamber when none heard the expected thud of a fallen body or scream of a dying victim. Yaro leaned forward, peering into the dim depths below. Instead of a broken body atop the pile of corpses, he saw the girl lowered unharmed to the floor by the arms of a giant who had caught her as she fell. He heard her shriek, "Our god is dead, is dead!" as she stared through the archway wherein the headless serpent lay. He watched as the giant recovered the bloodstained sword he had cast aside to catch the falling girl and as, with a smaller man beside him, the intruder vanished into the darkness.

As Conan and Subotai raced for the stair, the shocked moment of silence erupted into a clamor of confusion. By the time they reached the top step, they saw between the pillars several robed figures bending over the supine body of a dissheveled woman. Conan looked in vain for Valeria; he saw that the woman on the floor was raven-haired and so could not be the she-thief.

"Make for the tower shaft!" panted Subotai, and the two sprinted for the grating that separated the great hall from the tower well.

"The intruders!" shouted Yaro behind them. "There go the infidels! Slay them, ye faithful!"

The mob pressed forward, robes billowing. Among them came Yaro, two shaven-headed archers, and a man armed with an axe. Conan and Subotai squeezed through the grating.

"Where in the nine hells is the wench?" snarled Conan.

"Go on, you two!" cried a familiar voice. "I'll cover your retreat."

"Come on!" shouted Subotai, setting foot on the lowest rung of the ladder. Reluctantly, Conan sheathed his sword and, seizing the rung, followed his friend upward. The two archers reached the tower well and, kneeling down, nocked their arrows and drew their bowstrings back.

Suddenly a small, robed figure leaped forward and slashed the taut bowstrings. An instant later, one archer lay sprawling in his gore, with two of the faithful at his side. Bloody dagger in hand, Valeria threw off her stolen disguise and ran for the rope.

"Seize her!" bellowed Yaro.

The axe-man pushed after the fleeing girl and swung his weapon. Valeria ducked, and the force of his blow spun the fellow halfway round. Instantly, Valeria grasped her dagger with her teeth, whipped the rope's end around her adversary's throat, and tightened it.

As the man struggled, tearing at the rope that was strangling him, Valeria tied a quick knot and pushed the gasping man over the edge of the opening in the floor. Then, as the man spun into the black pit, the she-thief seized the other end of the rope, which passed over the pulley at the top of the tower. The weight of the falling body sent Valeria soaring effortlessly out of sight of the faithful who huddled, howling with frustration, at the bars of the grating.

As she hurtled upward, she passed Conan and Subotai, who were struggling painfully, hand over hand, up the narrow rungs of the iron ladder. Clinging to her rope with both hands, and gripping her dagger in her teeth, the girl threw back her head and laughed, as if to say, "Hurry, laggards, if you want to catch me!"

Moments later, the men, panting with exertion, reached the top of the shaft and found Valeria cleaning the blood from her mouth and dagger. They sank to the well-rim flooring to catch their breath.

"Well, did you get it?" asked Valeria.

Wordlessly, Conan pulled the ice-fire gem from his tunic and held it up to view. Her smile of satisfaction was brief; for sounds of pursuit billowed up from below. "They're climbing the ladder!" the girl whispered, peering down the long shaft. "I think some beast-men are among them. Hide the Serpent's Eye!"

"Get out on the parapet," said Conan, nodding toward the star-decked doorway. "I'll lop off their heads, one by one, as they reach this platform."

"No!" replied Valeria. "Too risky! Let's go down the tower wall before they cut my rope. But hurry!"

Soon the three, like flies upon a wall, were holding the rope and backing down the tower's face, grateful that the setting moon no longer marked their hasty passage.

All but the Cimmerian had reached the safety of the ground when a hideous face appeared above the battlements, and a knife-wielding, hairy hand slashed at the slender rope that had supported the fugitives' descent. Seeing the strands begin to part, Conan glanced briefly downward to locate the black surface of the reflecting pool. Reassured, he planted both feet firmly on the tower wall, gave a mighty heave with his strongly muscled legs, and launched himself in mid-air just as the rope gave way. Twisting his lithe body like a falling cat, he plunged, unharmed, into the dark water.

Valeria laughed as Conan emerged unscathed; and her laughter echoed the angry cries from a growing number of observers on the battlements.

"Fools!" she explained. "They've aided our escape! Now none can descend to hinder our flight from these most foul confines!"

Chuckling, Subotai coiled the rope and slung it over his shoulder, then followed Conan and Valeria over the garden wall to the anonymity of the darkling city streets.

VIII

The Mission

Fire roared on the stone hearth of a dingy tavern in the Thieves' Quarter of Shadizar. The pungent smoke that curled, like a lazy cat, against soot-blackened rafters did not dim the rainbow brilliance refracted by the hundred polished facets of the Serpent's Eye. Three cloaked figures, hunched conspiratorially around the rubiate gem as it lay on the rough oak table, shielded it with their bodies from the casual observation of strangers.

"By Nergal, but it's beautiful!" sighed Subotai, as his greedy eyes feasted on the glittering jewel.

"That it is," drawled Valeria. She raised her wine goblet to her lips without diverting her attention from the object of her admiration.

"It had better be beautiful," growled Conan. "It all but cost the lot of us our lives."

Subotai grimaced fastidiously. "Must you awaken sleeping memories?" he asked. "A peril past is a danger best forgotten, as we say in Hyrkania."

Nevertheless, the little man began to recount the events which followed their discovery in the temple of the Tower of the Black Serpent. He recalled how they had clambered over the temple garden wall, while others of the cultists, alerted by their brethren upon the battlements, poured forth in a torrent of fury from an unseen door of the obscene place of worship. He reminded his companions of their day of hiding, too fearful of pursuit even to seek food in the local shops, and of how, at last, they made their way, gawking like newcomers to the city, to the lawless quarter whither few honest men or officers of the peace dared to seek out thieves and murderers. Sighing, Subotai squeezed shut his eyes to banish the painful memories. Then opening them, he feasted on the gorgeous gem as on a royal banquet.

"It was worth it," he murmured. "Think, Cimmerian, shall we have two dukedoms in Aquilonia, two emirates in Turan, or a pair of adjacent satrapies down in Vendhya? And on what, Lady Valeria, do you expect to spend your share of the fortune from the gem?"

"First we have to find a buyer for so valuable a jewel," murmured Valeria, glancing warily about. The tavern was a beehive of red-faced, sweating men, bawling out hoarse songs and thumping their mugs on the rude table-tops, while a naked dancer, her oiled body gleaming in the firelight, undulated to the barbaric rhythm of the music.

"You had no trouble disposing of the stones you prised from the tower battlements," observed the little thief, with a meaningful nod at Valeria's wallet, abulge with gold coinage stamped with the bearded profile of Osric, King of Zamora. The girl, pressing the purse closer to her side, mistrustfully eyed the merrymakers, a crowd of whores, highwaymen, pimps, mercenaries, and off-duty guardsmen.

"Lower your voice, idiot, before you attract attention," she snapped, the pupils of her eyes glinting like a pair of daggers.

Subotai shrugged. A lean-shanked serving boy sidled over, gathering up empty flagons; and the Hyrkanian, nudging the Cimmerian's knee, caught the boy's arm.

"Find us girls, lad, sleek girls with round hips and pointed teats! Having explored the horizons of the world, I now intend to explore the limits of the fleshly pleasures, for which I have waited long—too long."

The youth, with a knowing leer, bent to whisper directions in the Hyrkanian's ear. Conan and Valeria exchanged a long and meaningful look.

"Well, comrade. I'm off to Madame Ilga's house for a

night of well-earned revelry. What are your plans? And yours, Lady Valeria?"

"As for the two of us, we have—other plans," said Conan, gruffly. Subotai grinned, eyeing two pairs of hooded eyes.

"So, it's like that, is it? I thought as much! Well, joy to you both, my friends; I now bid you a fond goodnight. Every man has his weakness; I intend to exercise mine assiduously. I leave you to practice your own."

Valeria caught his sleeve, as the Hyrkanian lurched unsteadily to his feet, prepared to venture forth into the night. She handed him a portion of the wealth contained in the plump pouch.

"Be wary, little man! Remember: a man of means has many boon companions, but few true friends."

Subotai scoffed at her temerity. "I have killed men before this—men who have had eyes in the backs of their heads, like that monstrosity atop the tower, young Conan! Besides, this gold was far too dearly bought for me to squander it on others' satisfactions. I intend to spend it entirely on myself!"

With a careless wave of his hand, the bowlegged man strutted off through the crowd toward the nighted street beyond the tavern door. Conan met Valeria's thoughtful stare with eyes that burned a volcanic blue. "Let's seek the comfort of our room, girl."

Valeria smiled at the intensity of the barbarian's desire, for it was every bit as ardent as her own. For a long moment, she fondled the roseate gem in a sensual way, then slipped it into her bosom and followed Conan from the inn.

A crippled hag led Conan and Valeria into the candlelit interior of a hut, leering at them with a toothless grin. Conan flicked her a small coin, and, bowing, she scurried from the room. The barbarian doffed his tunic as the she-thief unbuckled her belt and body armor.

Kneeling, Valeria ran her hungry hands over Conan's naked body. "Tell me," she breathed, "one thing—only one. When first I saw you, in the shadows, you moved so beautifully—where did you learn to move that way?"

Conan touched her breasts and ran a hand across her tight stomach and mobile hips.

Valeria gasped in ecstasy, holding herself taut as his seeking hands slid over her quivering body. "Where did you learn to move like that?"

For a moment, Conan studied the eager girl, his face impassive; then, putting his hands to his scarred neck, revealed the marks of the cruel collar he had worn. Valeria kissed the scars with frenzied kisses and threw herself upon him in a convulsion of sexual pleasure. Then undulating in his embrace, she tossed back her long hair and showed him identical scars. She, too, had endured long nights as a Pit fighter. Then the candle flickered out, and the darkness echoed with small sounds of happiness.

Dawn found the lovers in the low-ceilinged common room of the poor tavern, eating hungrily. Conan carved a steaming slab of meat from the spit and proffered it to Valeria on the point of his dirk. The girl gnawed the fragment with enthusiasm, as grease trickled down her chin; while Conan carved off a larger piece of meat to sate his rapacious appetite.

Conan never forgot this tender encounter. Many years later, he told his scribe: "If the gods do practice love, can it be greater? No woman before her or since could be her equal—but of this I had no knowledge at the time."

They washed the meat down with wine, cooled in snow carried from the mountaintop—a beverage for lordlings. Drunk with loving as much as with strong drink, Valeria leaned against the rough settle, and watched Conan as he ate, admiring the coiled springs of his muscles as they moved beneath his skin like the musculature of a splendid animal.

He, for his part, admired the woman's sensuous beauty, as she sat in repose before the embers of the fire, her garments, disarrayed, revealing her fair neck and shoulders. Conan had discovered a small hole drilled in the upper end of the great jewel, the Serpent's Eye, and through it he had threaded a narrow thong so that, wearing it, she would minimize the chance of losing it. Now its unearthly fires sparkled against the rondure of her breasts, doubling their beauty.

As the morning waned, Subotai, who had been carried back to the inn by Madame Ilga's grinning slaves, recovered from his debauch, amid groans and protestations of repentance. Before the sun had set, the three thieves once more embarked on a fresh round of pleasure and diversion. Their shabby garments had been replaced by leather jerkins and fine furs; their crude ornaments of iron had been exchanged for rings and armlets of polished bronze and gleaming silver, wrought by skilled craftsmen; good boots of fine leather had taken the place of their outworn buskins; and, with the aid of the Hyrkanian, Conan had selected knives and swords from the booth of a master smith.

This finery, together with the hearty meals and evenings' entertainments, were bought with monies from the jewels Valeria had purloined from the battlements of the tower. The circumspect conspirators did not, as yet, attempt to sell the snake stone, for they knew that spies and informers of the snake cult would be aprowl through the bazaars of Shadizar, eager to claim their holy talisman. In Turan, perhaps, or down in Vendhya, they hoped to find a merchant with sufficient means to buy the jewel and sufficient caution to say nothing of his purchase.

Despite their unaccustomed wealth, the three companions soon tired of their life of leisure. Wrestlers, dancing girls, and feasts—all became stale and vitiated pleasures to survivors of a life wherein danger honed an edge of zest to every moment snatched for comfort or amusement. All too soon came their deliverance from boredom; and it caught them unprepared.

One evening, as the three lolled, half-drunk and half-asleep, over their cups in the darkened tavern to which they had repaired once they found they could afford better accommodations, Valeria was roused from her stupor by the glint of a spear blade reflected in the firelight. Her half-uttered cry galvanized the others into action. They saw their table rimmed about by grim-faced soldiers arrayed in breastplates of gilt and bronze, and heavy, polished helmets set low on their brows.

Conan, instantly awake, half-rose from his chair.

Thinking these intruders guardsmen from the serpent-temple who had tracked their thievery down, he sought a means of escape. But no, the soldiers bore on helm-crest and cuirass the royal sigil of Zamora; these were legionnaires of the King.

"What do you want with us?" Conan grunted, eyeing the men with dour suspicion. "We have been carousing, true, but surely that is not against the Royal Law. . . ."

"Up and come with us, the three of you!" snapped an officer. "All questions will be answered by those who have dispatched us to seek you out. Let's have no trouble now!"

Subotai, still plunged in drunken stupor, looked at the leveled spear blades. Twisting his features into an obsequious smile, he muttered, "Aye, no trouble . . . no trouble at all . . ." Clinging to the table for support, he reeled to unsteady feet.

Perforce they accompanied the armed men; to draw a sword would have been suicide, despite their fighting skills. Alone, Conan might have chanced the odds of one man against twelve; but his burgeoning love for Valeria disarmed him. He would not risk her harm, though freedom itself hung in the balance.

Under a moonless sky, they trudged through silent streets, deserted at this hour even by footpads and other creatures of the night. At last they came to a wide avenue, at the end of which the spired bulk of the royal palace rose black against the brilliance of the stars. At the officer's command, a gate in the peripheral wall swung open. The squad of soldiery marched the three adventurers beneath pillared arcades and along graveled walks set amid smooth velvet lawns and marble fountains, whose opulence of water filled the night with music.

As the group reached the main portal of the palace, Subotai—a traveled man—eyed the architecture with appreciation. The abode of the Zamoran king was reputed to be one of the most exotic edifices east of Aquilonia, built as it was on the profits of trade with the Far East. But, as they passed the guards, standing stiffly before the doorway, his sharp eyes spotted vestiges of decay—cracks in the masonry and marks of dampness. He shrewdly guessed that all the vast wealth of this monarchy could not combat some

crawling inner rot, some cancer gnawing at the guts of the
state, even as the insidious tendrils of the serpent cult
sapped the courage and resolve of the citizenry.

Conan, less given to philosophy, shot keen glances to
the left and right as they were led along a maze of halls and
curving marble stairs. Seeking to orient himself in case they
might need to battle their way to freedom, he little heeded
the carven balustrades of ivory and alabaster, the rich wall
hangings, the silk-upholstered benches and curiously-
wrought torchères, which spelled a luxury of living beyond
his wildest imaginings. And yet at length it was borne in
upon him, even in the subdued light of the lamps and
candles, that these fine furnishings were not in pristine
condition. There were tears in the tapestries, stains on the
carpets, and gilding peeling from the ornate furniture, as
though from long neglect.

The grand hall of the palace, for all its sculptured
surfaces, echoed as emptily as a burial vault. Footsteps
reverberated through the gloom; dust lay heavy on the floor
tiles. As the adventurers and their escort approached the
throne of Zamora, they perceived a figure shadowed by the
canopy, brooding hand on chin, whose eyes bespoke a
warrior long lost to wine and decadence and sloth. Beside
the lone figure stood a single servant, who conversed in
whispers with his superior.

Conan saw that King Osric, for such the manner and
address of the captain of the guard proved him to be, was a
man sapped of vigor and devoid of hope. His age rested
heavily on his sagging shoulders. His lined face testified to
a life of care and disappointment.

A soldier laid the weapons of the captured adventurers
below the king's feet as the captain, dropping to one knee,
said, "The thieves whom you requested, Sire."

Subotai and Valeria, knowledgeable in the ways of
royalty, bowed low; Conan faced the king impassively.

A guardsman, poking the barbarian in the ribs, hissed,
"Bow, oaf!" Conan shot the man a slit-eyed scowl, but he
managed a jerky nod.

The monarch looked at the prisoners with an absent
eye, his mind elsewhere. At last he roused himself, and
with a flip of a finger, indicated that his officer should rise.

To clothe the stark silence, the man endeavored to jog the royal memory. "These are the thieves who robbed the Tower of the Serpent."

Then, in a hoarse voice, quivering with emotion, the monarch spoke: "Know you what you have done, thieves? You have caused him to come before me, before my very throne—Yaro, the black priest—to intimidate me, nay, to threaten Osric, High King of all Zamora! What insolence! What arrogance! These priests of the Black Serpent who set themselves above the monarchs of the world! And it is you, three thieves, gutter scum, who have brought this to pass!"

Conan shot a sidewise glance at his companions. Valeria wet her lips in nervous apprehension. Subotai's keen eyes darted like those of a cornered rat, seeking for an exit. The barbarian tensed, gathering his strength for an explosion of violence. Unarmed, he harbored no illusions about the outcome; but better to sell his life dearly than to present a willing neck to axe or knotted rope. He might take a guard or two with him into the black beyond.

The King continued staring at the thieves; but now a smile tugged at the corners of his bearded lips. Brushing aside his velvet robe, he rose to his feet, crying: "Thieves, I salute you! It was a noble deed you did!" The king barked a short laugh. "You should have seen the black priest's face! So furious was he that foam dribbled from his lips! I have not more enjoyed a sight since the night when I was wed!"

Then, turning to his bodyguards, he added: "Fetch stools for my larcenous friends, Captain Kobades. You shall remain, but as for you others, back to your duties! And bring some wine—wine of the best vintage."

A page brought silver goblets and a beaker of fine red wine; and there, standing before the throne of Zamora, they drank to the King's health, and he raised his cup to theirs. Subotai, bewildered at this sudden turn of fate, greedily imbibed his potion; Valeria and Conan, more accustomed to adulation after Pit-fighting successes, responded with better grace.

"You may be seated," said the King at last. He stared into his wine cup, brooding. When he spoke, his words were disjointed, his voice querulous.

"This man Thulsa Doom—long have I chafed at the presence of this demigod in my poor kingdom. Snakes in my beautiful capital! To the west, to the south, in Brythunia, Corinthia, everywhere snakes! Everywhere these black towers with their black-hearted priests! They steal away our children and turn them into monsters—into reptiles like the snakes they worship. Our corrupted young raise their envenomed fangs against their very parents. . . ."

Trembling, Osric buried his face in his hands. The three companions looked at one another, then turned to stare at Captain Kobades. The king perceived their glances.

"My own guards dare not stand against them. My bravest warriors, my fiercest fighting men shrink from their duty, fail in their sworn allegiance. You alone, you guttersweepings, have dared to beard Yaro in his citadel!

"All who stand against the serpent priests are set upon and slain. Death in the night . . . have you seen aught of this?"

At a signal, the monarch's servant handed him a thin bronze-handled dagger with a blade that undulated like the body of a serpent. Holding it in his outstretched palm, the king continued:

"Here is the serpent's fang, thrust into my father's heart by his younger son, my brother, who has been ensorcelled by their witchcraft. And my own daughter, the jewel of my kingdom, the joy of my old age, has likewise fallen under the spell of Thulsa Doom. She has turned against me and the elder gods. Does she bear a dagger such as this, pointed at my heart? Is this the fate awaiting me?"

Conan scowled, remembering the exquisite beauty of the young woman in the veiled palanquin. Subotai had told him she was the daughter of the king, but the barbarian found it difficult to believe that a girl so lovely might someday murder her own sire, although he knew that she was a priestess of the serpent god.

With a sudden explosion of anger, King Osric hurled the serpentine dagger to the marble floor, where it lay, a thing of evil exposed for all to see. "Each generation is weaker than the one before. Today's young wallow in this snake cult—this false religion. They yearn to be slaves and beggars, drugged dreamers. When I was young, boys strove to be heroes, not parasites and destroyers."

The King looked down, a weak old man beset by problems that he could not solve. Tremulously, he said: "Now I must call on thieves to save my kingdom!"

Valeria, with unaccustomed pity in her voice, directed a question at the rambling monarch. "What is it that you want of us, Sire?"

"My daughter, my little Yasimina—she follows him wherever he goes . . . Yaro, I mean, Yaro the black priest. She says she seeks the truth in the depths of her soul. . . . These addle-pated fools forget the old strengths, the old virtues. They wallow in depravity, as hogs wallow in mud, and call it a religion!

"And at this very moment, my daughter travels eastward to meet the man called Doom in the mighty stronghold of his cult, the center of his web of intrigue. Go you to the Mountain of Power and steal her back for me!"

The king gestured; and at the wordless command, the servant bore an urn from the shadows and tipped the vessel. Out spilled a dazzling flood of gems, to rattle to the floor before the adventurers' feet—rubies, amethysts, topazes, sapphires, and winking diamonds. A second kingly gesture stemmed the flow. Valeria gasped; greed shone in the Hyrkanian's eyes. Conan, suspecting a trick, stood staring at the king.

"Go on, pick them up," urged Osric. "They'll do for an earnest. With them you can buy weapons and horses. You can hire mercenaries to fight for you. Fetch my Yasimina back, and you shall be given all the gems remaining in that jar. Show them, Vardanes!"

The servant proffered the vessel, whereupon Subotai thrust in a finger and felt around. Satisfied that the jar had no false bottom and that myriad jewels remained, the Hyrkanian nodded and withdrew his inquiring hand. With Valeria, he swept up the fallen stones and placed them in a wallet.

Conan watched his companions scramble to retrieve the gems; then, frowning thoughtfully, he addressed the King: "Why is it that you do not fear a dagger in the dark, or poison in your cup?"

Osric smiled a bitter smile. "There comes a time, my friend, when, even for kings, gems cease to sparkle, gold's luster dims, and food and drink lose all their savor. A time when the very throne room, however gilded, becomes a prison cell. Then all that remains is a father's love for his child. But you . . . what would you know of that? You are too young, too full of life.

"When my end comes, at the hand of Doom or any other, I shall not greatly mind, if only my child be free of this curse and able to serve my people as their queen."

Conan nodded. "Very well, King Osric, I will slay this Doom or die in the attempt—I have my own score to settle with him. If I can rescue your daughter, I'll do that, too."

"We are then in accord!" said the King, and added to his captain of the guard, "Show my guests to the chambers prepared for them. See to their comfort. Fare you well!"

The three followed Captain Kobades from the shadow-haunted room, leaving Osric brooding on his dais.

IX

The Road

For two days after their audience with King Osric, the adventurers went to bed bone weary. Many preparations had to be made in haste—dried foods, skins of wine, bedding, and a hundred other things were needed for the journey. Jewels had to be bartered for coins of gold, silver, and humble copper. Then there was the matter of the horses.

One morning Conan and Valeria strolled about the horse market while Subotai, the only experienced horseman among them, haggled over their mounts. Once Conan drew Subotai's attention to a spirited stallion, which pranced at the end of its tether and rolled a wicked eye.

"That's the one for me!" exclaimed Conan.

The Hyrkanian chuckled. "Just how long do you think you would sit that steed? Since you have never been astride any nag, let me find you one that is safe and slow and big enough to bear your weight."

Conan spent hours learning to ride the beast that Subotai selected for him. Under his friend's tutelage, he learned how to walk, trot, and gallop, and how to saddle, curry, and feed the animal. Once, when a tumbleweed, driven by the wind, startled the horse, it moved with unexpected suddenness and threw its rider. Cursing, the barbarian picked himself up and set about catching his mount.

"I told you to use your knees!" admonished Subotai. "Never mind; if that's the worst tumble you ever take, you'll be luckier than most. We Kerlaits say a man is not a horseman until he has had seven falls."

That evening, as Conan sat in the bedchamber nursing his sore muscles, two of the king's servants hauled in a large wooden tub. Other attendants appeared with buckets of steaming water. When they withdrew, Valeria stripped off her clothes and stepped into the tub with a sigh of contentment.

"Come on in!" she said. "There's room for both of us."

Conan shook his head. "Hot baths are unhealthy. Steam damages the lungs."

"Rubbish! I've had hot baths all my life, and look at me! Besides, you don't smell like attar of roses. I'll scrub your back for you."

Still the barbarian refused. "Later, perhaps, when you are done."

The girl sat in the tub, scrubbing her slender limbs. Suddenly she turned to Conan. "To hell fires with Doom and the princess, both! The man is evil—a sorcerer who can summon demons from the nether pits, things like that which you slew on the parapet. As for the princess, why should we save her if she wants to die in his service? Let her reap the results of her folly!

"Besides, 'tis said this Mountain of Power, Doom's fortress, cannot be breached. It houses thousands of his followers. What chance have we against so many?" She stood up. "Throw me that towel, will you?"

Bathed and dried, Valeria lay back on the huge bed, toying with her fistful of gems. She watched the firelight flicker across their polished surfaces as she let them trickle between her fingers, cascade down the cleft between her high breasts, and spill across her belly. Then she continued: "I've spoken to Subotai, and he agrees. We'd be fools to undertake so perilous a mission. Let us take what we have whilst we still have our lives! Forget Doom and his silly princess! What the king has given us, together with the gold we'll surely get when we sell the Serpent's Eye, will make us rich . . . able to live like gentlefolk."

Conan sat on the edge of the bed, his thoughts in-turned, his back to the girl. Valeria crawled over to him, spilling the jewels upon the coverlet. She ran a caressing hand across his broad shoulders, kissed the nape of his neck, and, sliding her arms about his chest, pillowed her head on his shoulder.

Seemingly oblivious to Valeria's beguilements, Conan sat motionless, staring at his closed fist.

"Never have I had so much as now," the she-thief murmured dreamily. "All my life I've been alone. Often I've stared into the open jaws of death, with none to care whether I lived or died. Alone in the cold and dark, I've peered into the huts and tents of others, and seen the warm glow of firelight and men and women sitting side by side, with their young playing at their feet. But I walked the world . . . alone."

She looked at Conan's face, but found it dark and somber.

"Now I have you. We have warmth and passion and love. And we are rich. We need never face perils again in the getting of gold. Let us sit together with a lighted lamp to banish darkness. Let some other lonely person look in and envy us. . . ."

Valeria reached out, scooped up a handful of bright jewels, and poured them playfully down his naked chest. "Come, let us live!"

Wordlessly, Conan shook his head. Then slowly he opened his clenched hand. On his palm rested the bronze medallion taken from the altar of the serpent-god—the plaque that bore the sigil of Doom, two snakes facing each other upholding a black sun.

Dawn tiptoed into Shadizar, turning the spires of the royal palace into rose and gold. Entering the chamber where Valeria lay sleeping, the tender morning light aroused her from her dreams. Sleepily, she threw back the silken coverlet and stretched her nude limbs in sensuous enjoyment of the sun's warm kisses. Then she reached out to touch the naked body of her lover, but nobody lay beside her. Conan was gone.

Instantly she was wide awake, staring at the empty pillow. Instead of the magnificent form of the young barbarian, she saw only a handful of glittering stones, his share of the king's advance payment. Involuntarily, her hand sought her throat; the Eye of the Serpent still hung between her breasts. Her eager eyes searched the bedchamber; Conan's gear and clothing had vanished. A tear rolled down her cheek and was instantly wiped away. Pit fighters don't cry, she told herself sternly.

Far to the east of Shadizar, a lone rider picked his way through a pass in the Kezankian Mountains, where the foothills reach the stone-strewn steppe of northernmost Turan. It was Conan, but not the penniless runaway slave who once before traversed this forbidding land. The huge barbarian was now clad in fine rainment, with a tunic of mesh-mail over his clothing. He bore a steel cap on his head. At his side hung the ancient sword that he had taken from the cave of the grinning skeleton, now whetted to a razor edge and thrust into a splendid scabbard of reptile skin. To guard against the chill winds of early spring, he wore above his mailshirt a cloak of well-tanned wolfskin.

Remembering the past, he rubbed the coarse black beard that shadowed his scarred face. The Pitmaster Toghrul had compelled his fighters to shave, lest they present their opponents with an advantage, and Conan had continued in this habit. But now, eager to come to grips with Doom, he had ignored the practice.

The Cimmerian remembered, too, the lovely woman from whose encircling arms he had departed. Many years later, he told his scribe, *I knew Valeria would never understand. Her gods were not the northern gods. I turned east, but bowed my head to Valhalla. Crom awaited my vengeance upon my enemies with calm indifference. I knew my life hung on a slender thread, but I had no other course.*

For days on end he rode along a narrow trail made festive with a profusion of wildflowers, red, blue, lavender, and yellow. Sometimes he bent low in the saddle to shield himself against a sudden storm, while winds and mountain-born sleet tore at his weather-ravaged face. From time to time, he paused to give the ponderous gelding Subotai had selected for him a few hours of grazing on the sparse vegetation.

Whenever Conan feared that he might have strayed from his true path, he questioned those he met along the road: a lone shepherd, a ragged, toil-worn peasant, a nomad driving a creaking wagon crammed with his household goods, while his wife and sons herded his starveling cattle before him. Ever they directed him further to the east.

One toothless peasant looked blankly at the imposing figure on his enormous steed. Conan showed him the symbol of the snake cult, the sigil of Doom. The light of comprehension lit the besotted face, and the man responded, "Many go—children mostly—they travel this way." He motioned with a weathered hand; then, reversing the direction, he added, "None travels back again."

One day the Cimmerian picked up a trail made by many feet. He quickened his pace and, before sundown, saw a gray plume of dust staining the cerulean sky. Warily, he approached, keeping the dust cloud in sight; and at length he overtook the source of the unwonted cloud. As he expected, it was a long procession of pilgrims headed for the sacred environs of Set, the snake god. Bedraggled youths and maidens, decked with wreaths and garlands of long-dead flowers, plodded along, beating tambourines and singing their monotonous chants.

Conan rode past them, eyeing the column watchfully. One or another of the votaries called out to him as he rode past, saying: "Come, O warrior! Join with us! Throw away your sword and give yourself to time, to the earth, as we have done! Yield to fate! Come with us to the Mountain of Power!"

Smiling grimly, Conan shook his head and cantered on. Time enough to give oneself to the earth when life has fled, he thought.

The trail sloped upward to a pass between two ridges of volcanic rock; and beyond them, on a level plain, a conical peak loomed high against the sky. In the distance Conan could see the shimmering blue waters of the Vilayet Sea, which reached to the horizon. From his high vantage point, the barbarian perceived another column of trudging pilgrims, half hidden in a cloud of dust, their rhythmic chanting carried to him on the ambient air.

Conan paused on the uplands to breathe his mount and study the landscape that stretched before him in the lush greenery of its springtime foliage. Along the shores of the great inland sea, to the right of the Mountain of Power, lay a stretch of broken country from which thrust up a series of mounds. Abandoning the path beaten by the shambling feet of many pilgrims, Conan urged his nag toward the broken ground half a league south of the mountain. When he came among them, he recognized the mounds as tumuli of the sort in which some primordial peoples were wont to bury their kings. Dominating the rest, one extensive mound rose to the height of several men and pressed outward to the width of half a bowshot. Around the base at intervals were set a row of pointed stakes; and on each he saw impaled the remains of a horse and mounted rider. Wind and weather had reduced most to simple skeletal states, decked only in bits of faded cloth and the remains of iron armor.

Conan circled the heaped-up earth warily, a prickling of uncanny premonition roughening his hide. He could not tell how long the ghastly company had stood on guard in this forgotten place, but there was something in his barbaric soul that cowered before the undead and unknown.

On the far side of the mounds, he came upon an area of tumbled masonry and broken stones, the shards of a city ruined long ago. He paced his horse among the shattered columns, toppled slabs, collapsing walls, rubble-filled ditches, and ghosts of wells waterless for eons past. The devastation seemed complete, its cause beyond man's understanding.

Then to his astonishment, Conan sighted a shabby hut, scarcely more than a lean-to of sticks bound into a frame covered with the hides of wild animals. Before the entrance of tattered skins, a small fire burned, wafting the pungent smoke of roasting meat into the sea air. As the Cimmerian reined his beast to gaze in wonder at this habitation, a gaunt graybeard in worn and dirty robes appeared to stare uncertainly at the intruder.

"Hail, grandfather!" growled Conan, raising an empty hand to signal his intentions. "I come in peace."

"And well it is you do!" the oldster replied with an energy of manner that belied his wrinkled age. Shaven-headed, flat-faced, ill-clad though he was, in some strange way he commanded the barbarian's respect. "Know, young warrior, that I am a wizard, and that this necropolis contains the bones of mighty kings and their restless spirits. He who harms my living flesh must deal with forces that he knows not of."

"Can you summon demons, wizard?" A note of jocundity appeared in the barbarian's voice.

"Aye, that I can! A devil fiercer than any other in the seven hells!" The old man's boast ended in a fit of coughing.

"How fortunate, then, that we shall be friends," said Conan. He tossed a silver coin to the wizard, who caught it with notable agility. "That should pay for a few days' board at this, your inn."

At sunset, Conan, having doffed his helm and mail, sat before the fire, gnawing on a piece of smoked meat and unleavened bread. The hermit bustled about, offering his guest a gourd of sour ale and gabbing as if had had no converse in years.

"These burial mounds have been here since the days of the Titans, stranger," the old man said. "Great kings sleep here, kings whose realms once glittered like lightning on a windy sea. And curses lie beneath those piles of earth; that is why I dwell below their summit."

"Are you the caretaker of this graveyard, then?" inquired Conan.

The wizard laughed. "Nay, but I sing to those who lie here, to lull their slumbers . . . tales of old, of battles fought and heroes made, of riches and of women."

"How do you live, good wizard?"

"The neighboring country folk bring me flesh and bread; and I cast spells and tell fortunes for them. I raise a few tubers and greens, besides. No one molests me; they know my powers and position."

Conan dipped his shaggy head towards the Mountain of Power. "What about them?"

"The serpent-besotted fools? They know me well. But, thinking me mad, they do not bother me. Each spring the man named Doom comes hither to make sacrifice to the ghosts of my sleeping kings. You've seen them. . . ." He gestured towards the skeletal remains of men astride their horses. Conan, unsure whether the bones were those of ancient kings or of Doom's followers, ate in silence for a space.

"Do any wild flowers bloom hereabouts?" he asked.

The old man's jaw hung slack. "Flowers? What on earth . . . ?" Then, recovering his composure, he said, "Yes, I suppose you can gather a few. A month ago the plain was carpeted with them. What do you want with flowers?"

"You'll see," said Conan.

The next morning Conan arose, shaved off his recent growth of beard, and brought out from his bag of gear the white robe of a pilgrim. Thus clad, he spent an hour prowling the outskirts of the ruined city, plucking the sturdiest flowers he could find. When, after breaking his fast, the barbarian began to weave the blossoms into a wreath, the wizard eyed him with distaste.

Unperturbed, Conan asked the ancient one: "What know you of this Thulsa Doom? Rest assured, I am not one of his."

Relief flooded the oldster's face, and he grinned a toothless grin. "Well, you don't look much like a pilgrim. If you mean to enter the mountain thus disguised, beware. Doom's people are deceivers, fierce and treacherous. Besides, you cannot wear that sword; even beneath your robe, they'd instantly perceive its presence."

"Well then, I must needs do without." Conan reached under his robe, unbuckled the baldric, and handed the scabbarded blade to the wizard, saying: "Keep it oiled, and find forage for my horse. I'll reward you well when I return . . . if I return."

Adjusting his wreath of drooping field flowers, Conan

strode away toward the mountain. The wizard, muttering protective cantrips, watched him go.

The road grew steep as it zigzagged up the side of the Mountain of Power. Conan, walking briskly, joined a straggling line of youths and maidens. Their features were haggard, their faces dusty, and their eyes vacant. So vast was the difference between the robust barbarian in his fresh garment and the weary, travel-stained band that Conan feared nothing could save him from discovery.

Along the winding way, girls in fresh robes called encouragement, chanting and waving the pilgrims onward. At the first bend in the road, Conan saw a small temple of white marble, which gleamed against the brooding obsidian on which it rested. This white shrine, the least of the Shrines of Doom, bore on its outer walls a frieze of writhing shapes, obscene and serpentine; beneath its swelling cupola all seekers must pass for cleansing and renewal.

At the arched entrance to the shrine, a woman stopped Conan to hand him a fresh garland, for the chaplet he had woven some hours before was already wilted. Bowing his head to receive the wreath, he prepared to move on; but the girl with upraised hand detained him. Panic seized him until he realized this was a ritual greeting.

"You must give up all that you hold, tall pilgrim," murmured the girl in a sing-song monotone. "You must see yourself in clear water, as you have never seen yourself before."

Copying the reply of the pilgrim who preceded him, Conan intoned, "I wish to be cleansed."

As the girl smiled vaguely at him, Conan became aware that she did not really see him, and he guessed that she was drugged. Unaware of his agitation, the girl hastened through the prescribed words, devoid as they were of warmth and meaning: "You are safe now from the perils of the road. We are all safe here in the shadow of the mountain. Fear no more; for this is the road to paradise!"

Conan mumbled an unintelligible reply and hastened forward. At the next turning of the road, he passed through a narrow cleft between two slabs of rock, and found himself in a natural amphitheater, a bowl-shaped area shielded from the wind. Tents and rude pavilions littered the rocky ground. On either side stood burly guards, proud and imposing in their armor of lacquered black leather; beyond them he saw, or thought he saw, black-robed priests from the Temple of the Serpent.

Instinctively, the Cimmerian drew back, then hastily assumed a vacant-eyed, slack-jawed expression. Attracted by his failure to move forward, a priestess hurried over. "Is something wrong?" she asked.

Conan gestured toward the faceless guards. "Who are they?"

"They are our friends. They are here to protect us."

"To protect us? Protect us from what?"

The priestess answered soothingly, as to a frightened child; "Very often from ourselves. Seldom do we know what is good for us; always are we beset with doubts and fears. We are so blind that rarely can we discern the path of truth. Only the Master can set our feet upon the path to paradise."

Gently taking his hand, she drew Conan to the rear of the procession of which he had been a part, and there she left him. Swept along with the rest, he found himself in a crowd of boys and youths, who were being herded into a long line by several priests and ordered to strip off their travel-stained garments. On the far side of the amphitheater, a line of women were vanishing from view.

The wily barbarian stood for a moment, undecided, among the bewildered throng. If he doffed his robe, the long dirk at his belt would instantly expose his imposture. As the line moved forward, he slipped between two tents and ran into a slender, robed and hooded priest.

"Whither go you, brother?" asked the man mildly.

"I . . . I know not," stammered the Cimmerian. "I fear . . ."

"You fear to bare yourself, eh lad! My boy, you should be proud of that splendid body." The priest reached out to touch him, but Conan fended off his hand. Undeterred, the priest continued, "How can you expect to reach the ultimate emptiness, my son, unless you have full knowledge of your body?"

Conan spied a cleft in the rocks well-shielded from public view.

"Can we not talk alone . . . where the others cannot see?" Conan motioned to the alcove. With a thin and knowing smile, the robed man bent his footsteps thither, saying, "We priests know much about the bodies and souls of men; you need feel no shame. . . ."

Once within the alcove, Conan turned. "Tell me," he asked with feigned innocence, "is the robe your only garment?"

"Aye, my son. It is all . . ."

"Good," grunted the barbarian and drove an elbow into the priest's ribs. As the bones cracked, only a strangled wheeze issued forth. Then a Pit fighter's hammer blow broke the man's neck.

A tall man in a hooded robe moved briskly through the line of naked pilgrims and headed for the temple. A priest, descending from the sanctuary, met his eyes and made a cryptic sign with his fingers. Conan clumsily mimicked the wordless greeting and, noting the look of puzzlement on the other's face, quickly moved on.

A pair of priests went by, deep in a fiery argument. Conan saw that on each breast hung a medallion like that which he had taken from the altar in the Serpent's Tower. Fumbling inside his unfamiliar robe, he brought forth his sigil and, despite its clumsy thong, placed it in view. The temple guards, rough, half-witted fellows with beetling brows, looked sharply at the false priest; then, seeing the medallion with its twin serpents, drew themselves to attention and let him pass. Thus Conan entered into the Mountain of Power.

X

The Mountain

Conan progressed along a passageway among other figures, little noticed, who drifted, mistlike, in the same direction. In time, the barbarian emerged into a courtyard of incredible beauty. Here were gardens bright with rainbow-tinted flowers, interlaced with strange, exotic trees. A fountain threw its crystal waters into a quiet pool, which was surrounded by marble benches.

Beyond the pool, he saw a ceremonial staircase, whose impressive risers led upward toward the portal of a temple. This doorway, splendidly embellished with marble carvings, led to a cavernous interior, hewn, Conan thought, from the living rock. In this vast sanctuary, the Cimmerian saw a semicircle of marble benches, row on row, backed by a walkway that was curtained, as it were, by a row of pointed columns, like obelisks.

Before the benches rose a dais, reached by a lesser flight of steps. Over the whole chamber a stained-glass dome filtered, from an unknown source of light, a radiance that rivaled that of the orb of heaven.

Beautiful women, clad in diaphanous veils, clustered about the steps of the dais, as reverent pilgrims sought seats among the welcoming benches. Conan, moving softly, joined the waiting throng; and reassured of his safety, he studied the subservient youths and maidens at his side. Their robes of fine fabrics and the brave ribbons on their brows marked them as beings above the common lot gathered outside the rock-hewn opulence he now enjoyed.

Presently, graceful young women brought trays of lighted candles and handed one to every votary. As the dome light dimmed, the slender tapers winked like stars in the nighted sky and, shining into the young faces of the worshipers, gave them the visages of gods.

Absorbed in this pageantry, Conan was unaware that two of the apelike sentinels followed him into the temple within the Mountain of Power. Now, in the deep shadows behind him, they held converse in sign language with the towering black priest, Yaro of Shadizar. Hither had come Yaro with his retinue to report the loss of the temple talisman, so that word of the theft could be trumpeted among the faithful in all the lands wherein the cult of the serpent god held sway. Here, too, Yaro hoped to discover the whereabouts of the purloiner and to prepare to apprehend him.

Summoned to the temple by the simian guards, the black giant studied the Cimmerian with narrow, thoughtful eyes. He had caught but a glimpse of the thief who had stolen the Eye of the Serpent, as Conan and Subotai scrambled up the narrow ladder to the top of the tower; but the burly shoulders, the swelling thews, the mane of coarse black hair hacked off at shoulder length were unmistakable.

The black priest turned to mutter a comment to another figure curtained by the darkness. As he moved forward, he proved to be a man of gigantic stature, wearing armor of blue steel backed by black leather; and on his breastpiece, in high relief, wriggled two serpents, intertwined.

Rexor, for it was he, had aged in the years since he had led the slave raid on the village of Conan's childhood and carried off the youth to toil long years at the Wheel. Yet the passage of time had somehow enhanced his presence and vitality. Strong beyond belief were the corded muscles that crawled down his naked arms, his massive thighs, his thickset neck. Free of the confining helmut, the brutality of the features appeared to have been refined by the passing years. Colder than ever were his eyes and deeper the lines

of cruelty about his thin-lipped mouth. The iron gray that
streaked the hair about his temples bespoke a man of steel.

His chill eyes took the measure of the Cimmerian
seated before him. He did not remember the child snatched
from his mother's side after her murder, but that did not
matter. Any intruder in the Temple of the Serpent was a
foeman; any uninitiated onlooker who observed the secret
rites was an impious and blasphemous infidel. And the
penalty was death, slow and painful death.

Conan's attention now was riveted on a procession of
priests, who marched with cadenced stride toward the dais.
Their deep-throated chanting swelled in volume as two lines
of naked girls, their bosoms draped with coiled serpents,
danced down the aisles to the blare of brasses and the clash
of cymbals. Behind them a group of Stygian priests bore
aromatic torches, which filled the air with undulating smoke
and a sweet, pungent odor. Behind them all came the catlike
figure of the man called Doom.

With eyes narrowed to smoldering slits, Conan stared
at his arch-enemy. Ignoring the magnificent fur-trimmed
robes, which swept behind Doom as he walked, the
barbarian youth focused on the evil face. The years had not
lessened the sensual allure of his hooded eyes and lean,
ascetic features, nor had time withered the seductive smile
with which he greeted his worshipers and the ecstatic
handmaidens who showered rose petals at his feet.

To Doom's left and a single step behind him, Conan
saw a young woman of breath-taking loveliness. Clad in a
gossamer gown that accented her voluptuous form and
golden flesh, she walked demurely, but the slumberous gaze
with which she caressed her master was shot through with
hidden fire. Conan grunted as he recognized the princess he
had glimpsed in the veiled palanquin on a street in Shadizar
—Yasimina, the missing daughter of King Osric.

While Yasimina knelt in humble adoration, Doom
stepped forward, raised his arms majestically, then abruptly
turned his palms down. The chanting ceased upon the
instant of the gesture. On the sepulchral silence that ensued,
his resonant voice rose and fell, like the tolling of a bell.

"Who amongst you fears the warm embrace of death?

When I, your father, ask it, will you take life for me? Will you strike true to the infidel heart, whether it be the heart of friend, or lover, or loved one in your former life?"

Pausing, he turned his hypnotic gaze on the entranced faces, upturned in ecstasy. "Doom!" they moaned, swaying in rhythm to the beat of his utterances. "Doom! Doom!"

The catechism went on. "Will you slip the silken noose over the heads of Set's enemies? In the wide world, will you stay true, ignoring the blandishments of the leaders, judges, and parents who have taught you falsely? Will you clutch the hilts of your daggers and spill the heart's blood of the infidels, to give them the infinite benison of eternal peace?"

Doom's magnetic eyes darted from face to face and held each follower in thrall. Now the questions ceased and the litany began.

"You will feel naught but joy when you perform your duty to your god and lord, when you strike for Set and Doom, when the infidel bows before the blade, the cord, or the bowstring, accepting the inevitable. You will grow in love of the Dark Master, the Wise Serpent, in the embrace of whose coils lies eternal life and bliss unutterable; for the day of Doom is at hand, the day of the Great Cleansing."

As the discourse proceeded, Doom's voice gained in intensity. He moved slowly down the dais steps and closer to his audience. With eyes transfixed, the votaries followed their leader's every move, until their unseeing gaze came to rest on Conan. The barbarian's primitive instincts alerted him to action, and he gathered himself for a leap to freedom.

"Your parents deceived you; your teachers deceived you. Fool others as they seek to fool you!"

Glaring directly at Conan, with hate-filled eyes, Doom shot out an accusing finger and addressed him:

"Infidel, you are deceived as you sought to deceive me. On this day you shall die."

Conan sprang to his feet, his teeth bared in a snarl. As he rose, footsteps crunched on the marble pave behind him; and alerted to danger, he whirled. Catlike though his

movement was, it was not quite swift enough; for even as
he pivoted, a heavy cudgel crashed down.

The blow, aimed at the nape of his neck, went slightly
awry and struck him on the temple. Although death was
thwarted, the massive impact sent the barbarian hurtling
into a spinning vortex of blackness, beyond the reach of
pain. He never felt the crushing blows that struck his inert
body, as the guards leaped upon him, snarling like wild
dogs. Boots thudded against Conan's ribs and belly while
merciless cudgels rose and fell, bludgeoning his face, his
torso, his helpless limbs. But he knew it not.

Consciousness returned haltingly, like an unwilling
schoolboy bending slow steps towards school. Each muscle
throbbed, as if every inch of flesh were one vast bruise.
Through half-open eyes, Conan saw the sun was shining
and dimly realized that a new day had dawned. Clenching
his jaw, he forced himself to test each limb and, half-
astonished, discovered none was broken. Although the
beating had been expert and thorough, it had not maimed or
crippled him.

At last he dared to open his swollen eyes. So blurred
was his vision that he mistook the sculptured fountain,
splashing its sprays of crystal water into rainbows, for a
dream. But as he glared from under tangled locks matted
with sweat and dried blood, he perceived paths of mosaics
meandering among beds of daffodils and tulips and all
manner of flowers that defied the painter's palette. Then he
knew he was lying in a garden in the sun. He noticed that a
high wall surrounded the garden and defined it, setting off
its color from the paler stone of the temple lieu beyond, the
so-called Mountain of Power, the stronghold of Doom.

With great effort, the Cimmerian raised his head an
inch or two above the pavement on which he lay. He saw
that the garden was tenanted by groups of youths and
maidens, some lounging atop the wall, some strolling
among the shrubs and flowers, and some seated by the
fountain at the feet of a towering figure who was busy
eating a ripe fruit. It came to Conan with a shock of
recognition that the man was Rexor, chief in command
under the supreme leader Doom.

A wave of nausea overcame the barbarian youth. He forced his aching body to its knees; the world swung dizzily about him; and he vomited. As he struggled to regain his feet, the clatter of chains made manifest to him that he was shackled, confined as he had been as a slave of the Wheel, and later as a Pit fighter. From broad bracelets and anklets locked about his limbs, strong chains were fixed to a bronzen ring set into the pavement.

Trembling with weakness, and overcome by despair, the once-mighty Cimmerian slumped to the ground and lay in his vomit. A pair of young votaries paused to look at the huddled form with an expression of distaste; the others continued past him, averting their indifferent gaze. As from a great distance, Conan heard their laughter carried on the gentle breeze.

How long he lay thus, Conan did not know; but at length Rexor strode over to him and barked: "The Master would speak to you now; and you, filthy swine, are unfit to come before him." So saying, Rexor stooped to unlock the manacles and, straightening up, pitched the half-conscious prisoner into the fountain. The sting of the icy water revived the battered youth enough so that, upon Rexor's command, he managed to crawl out of the basin to collapse on a marble bench.

A moment later the sibilant voice of Doom hissed in his ear; and looking up, Conan found the snake medallion suspended before his eyes.

"How came this plaque into your possession?" Doom asked in his sonorous voice. "Was it you who stole it from my house in Shadizar? And what befell the Eye of the Serpent—do you know who bore it off? Speak truth, and no further harm shall be your lot. Refuse, and pain—exquisite, ravishing—will carry your spirit into the ultimate ecstasy of death itself."

Conan spat a gobbet of bloody spittle, then, setting his jaw, stared in silence at his enemy. Doom considered him, his uncanny gaze boring into the barbarian's rebellious eyes as if to probe his very soul. At last, the cult leader sighed, shook his head, and pocketed the talisman.

Turning to his watchful lieutenant, Doom said: "His mind informs me that he gave the great jewel to some woman. For a few moments of pleasure, I have no doubt, caring not that it holds the key to the power of the world. Such a loss! Such animals have no understanding—no sense of the consequences of their actions."

Rexor growled, his voice thick with hidden anger, "I'll kill him for you, Master."

Doom shook his head, then turned back to the crouched and bloody form before him. In a voice devoid of anger, he said: "You broke into the house of my god, stole my property, murdered my servants, and slew my pets. You disrupted a ritual of importance to my followers; this grieves me most of all."

A spasm of some strange emotion briefly contorted the dark face of Doom, and the weird light of a nameless sorrow flickered within the depths of his burning eyes.

"You slew the great serpent coiled about my altar. Yaro and I are desolated by his loss; for we, ourselves, nurtured him from the egg. Why? Why did you steal my possessions and rob me of living things so precious to me? Why did you violate the sanctity of my temple and tamper with a ceremony your brutish mind could never grasp? Why have you invaded my very stronghold, and taken the life of a priest whom I called brother?"

"Had Crom granted me a few more minutes, I would have taken your life, too!" growled Conan through cracked and swollen lips.

"Why such hatred? Why?"

"You murdered my father and my mother. You slaughtered my people," muttered the barbarian. "You stole my father's sword of finely tempered steel. . . ."

"Ah, steel," Doom nodded, deep in meditation. "Many years ago I searched the world over for steel, for the secret of steel, which then I thought more precious than gold or jewels. Yes, I was obsessed by the mystery of steel."

"The riddle of steel," murmured Conan, remembering the words of his father, the Cimmerian smith.

"Yes, you know that riddle, do you not?" The cult leader's voice was intimate, persuasive. Speaking as to a friend, Doom's words continued emotionless, hypnotic, brimming with deceit. "In those days, I deemed steel stronger than all things, even than human flesh and spirit. But I was wrong, boy! I was wrong! The soul of man or woman can master everything, even steel! Look you, boy—"

Doom pointed to the walk along the top of the garden wall, whereon a lovely golden-haired girl held hands with a handsome youth.

"Fair, is she not, that beautiful creature? And the splendid boy beside her is her lover. Do you know what it is to love a girl, barbarian? Or to be truly loved by one?"

Remembering Valeria, from whom he had parted with such pain so many days ago, Conan's lips tightened, and he growled an assent deep within his throat.

"Perhaps you do," said Doom with the ghost of a smile. "Perhaps you think that love conquers all. But I will show you a force stronger than steel, or even than love. Watch closely now—"

Raising his hypnotic eyes, he fixed them upon the sweet face of the smiling girl above them on the wall.

"Come to me, child," he hissed, his sibilant voice scarcely above a whisper.

The childish face became suffused with joy. She poised for a moment at the edge of the embankment; then, without a glance at the youth beside her, she leaped from the wall and fell with a heavy thud on the tiles of the garden walk below.

Conan averted his eyes from the doll-like broken body near their feet. Doom laughed, the music of his laughter spun through with a note of triumph. Then he said: "That is strength, boy—that is power! It is strength against which the hardness of steel or the resilience of human flesh are as naught. What is steel, compared to the hand that wields it; what is the hand, without a mind to command it? There is the secret of strength. Steel, bah!"

Thulsa Doom paused and stared at Conan's impassive face. The barbarian's closed countenance, the set of his bruised shoulders seemed to the cult leader to diminish his power, to offer an unspoken insult to one unused to insults. He made one more attempt to reassert his authority and to impress the stubborn youth, whose body was in chains but whose soul remained free.

Doom raised a hand and caught the attention of the weeping lad who stood immobile, looking down at the broken body of the girl he loved. Doom's cruel lips curled, a movement noticed only by the keen-eyed Cimmerian, and a false smile lit his dark visage, as he whispered a command.

"Join her in Paradise, my son."

Without hesitation, moving like one walking in a dream, the boy unsheathed a small, jeweled dagger and plunged the sharp blade into his heart. The sun sparkled on the fountaining blood that poured from the wound, as the boy posed, statue-like, atop the wall. Then suddenly he crumpled and, pitching forward, fell dying on the body of the girl.

There was a look of triumph on the face of Thulsa Doom as he turned to regard the barbarian. "I have," he smiled, "a thousand more like them."

Conan, unimpressed, stared at him dourly. "What is it to me that you have power over fools and weaklings? You have never met a real man on equal terms and fought him face to face or hand to hand."

Fires of hate glowed in Doom's eyes, and something akin to shame flared for an instant and subsided under almost superhuman control. Conan, unheeding, continued:

"You slaughtered my people. You chained me to the Wheel of Pain, under the lash of the Vanir. You doomed me to be a slave fighting in the Pit, wondering whether each day would be my last. . . ."

Doom raised his dark head proudly. "Aye! And see what I have made of you, how life has toughened your flesh and hardened your spirit! Look at the strength of your will, your courage, your resolve to slay me to revenge your kin. You have followed me across the world, here to my innermost citadel of power, to avenge wrongs you fancy I have done you; whereas in reality I have made you a champion, a hero, a veritable demigod. And now, this gift of mine—this strength and courage and will, which I bestowed upon you through pain and suffering—you wish to waste on mere revenge. Such a waste! Such a pity!"

Doom, seeming truly grieved, chewed his underlip before continuing.

"I will vouchsafe you one last chance for life and liberty. Answer two questions: Whence got you the plaque of the twin snakes? Where is the Eye of the Serpent? Speak."

Conan silently shook his tousled head.

"Very well," Doom said at last. "You shall contemplate the fruits of your insolence on the Tree of Woe."

Turning abruptly on his heel, he started to leave the garden, while Rexor reappeared to take charge of the prisoner. Reaching the gate, Thulsa Doom turned once more to fling a command at his faithful lieutenant in his low, melodious voice.

"Crucify him," he said casually.

XI

The Tree

A red sun glared down upon a scene of desolation. A level plain of chalky soil, as white as new-fallen snow, stretched away in all directions. Above the ground, like sheeted ghosts, waves of heat danced a dance of death, shimmering in the motionless air; while from the barren soil, the traveler—had any ventured along this trackless waste—would have found his natural repugnance reinforced by the metallic smell of unfamiliar compounds.

Above this stark wasteland towered the Tree of Woe, a twisted, black monstrosity, with leafless branches clawing at the sky. Once, perhaps, it has been a noble shade tree, gentle to man and beast. Now it was a gaunt and spiny skeleton, a thing of evil.

High on the black trunk hung Conan the Barbarian. His naked body bore a powdering of chalk dust and dried blood, through which runnels of sweat carved their way. His tangled hair fell ropelike around his battered face, a cracked and sunburnt mask in which only the eyes lived. They were the angry, burning eyes of a trapped and dying beast.

Ropes, tightly bound, confined his arms to a pair of widespread boughs. Other ropes held his legs and thighs firmly against the rough bark of the tree. Cruel as were these thongs, far crueler were the pair of slender nails, whose square-cut heads pinioned the palms of his hands to the branches against which his arms were bound.

How many hours had passed since Doom's guards had inflicted this savage punishment upon him, Conan did not know. His mind was numbed by pain; his periods of rational consciousness intermittent. Thirst tormented him without respite; and the relentless rays of the sun tore at his burning flesh. Nothing broke the monotony of his agony save the shadows of vultures, drifting on lazy wings against the merciless sun, as they waited for him to die and furnish them a feast. These birds of prey seemed to be the only other living creatures in all the chalky waste.

One vulture floated near on slow-beating wings, and settled on a branch above the Cimmerian's head. It stretched its wattled neck to peer at the crucified man, whose head had sagged upon his broad breast. To the scavenger, the man's battered carcass seemed devoid of life. The vulture peered more closely, swiveling its head from side to side to bring first one, then the other eye to bear upon its prey.

Conan remained motionless. In a lucid moment, he had become aware that, without a sip of liquid, death would snatch him up before the sun had set. And there was only one thing he might drink on all the burning plain.

The vulture left its perch; and a solitary figure in a windless sky, it dipped, then gained altitude for its attack. As it swept in, its hooked beak poised for a stab at Conan's eyes, the bird's shadow fell across the Cimmerian's face. Summoning all his waning strength, Conan raised his head. He remained motionless when the vulture raked his chest, as, wings beating the air, the scavenger braced itself to lunge.

At that moment, Conan's head shot forward. His jaws snapped, wolflike, as his strong teeth sank into the bird's slender neck and choked off its squawk of surprise and pain. Black wings buffeted the barbarian's sunbaked face; claws raked his reddened flesh. But Conan's grip held fast, as he sank his teeth ever deeper into the wrinkled, featherless neck. There was a final crunch of breaking bone, and the vulture's wings hung limp. Keeping his jaws clenched,

Conan sucked the vulture's blood. Warm and salty though it was, the moisture rivaled a cup of the finest wine.

Somewhat revived, Conan raised his head once more. He saw that the sun, now declining in the west, had streaked the dreary plain with crimson. Suddenly, something about the scene brought the barbarian's dulled wits into focus. Was it a plume of dust, shot through with red from the setting sun, or was it a column of smoke? Whatever it might be, it was growing larger, moving closer.

For a long time, Conan could not make out the nature of the approaching object, which swam through ripples of heat like a swimmer breasting a wind-tossed sea. At length its irregular form coalesced into the figure of a man on horseback, riding at an easy canter. Abruptly, the horseman, riding as only a Hyrkanian could ride, urged his mount into a gallop. Despite his cracked and swollen lips, Conan grinned.

"Erlik! What have they done to you?" cried Subotai, leaping from his horse and tying the reins to a low branch of the blasted tree. Conan growled a reply, but so dry was his throat that no articulate sound issued forth.

With shaking hands, Subotai fumbled in his saddle bag and found an implement, a tweezer of the sort used to pull stones from the hooves of horses. Tucking it into his belt, he clambered up the tree trunk to the place where the Cimmerian hung. In frantic haste, he struggled to extract the nails from Conan's hands, hands that were swollen to twice their normal size. While the barbarian bit his lip to stifle his groans, Subotai wrenched and strained, until the nails came free.

Then, dropping the tweezer, the Hyrkanian sawed with his dagger at the ropes that bound Conan's legs; and, when those bonds were loosened, he slashed at the binding around his friend's arms.

"Hook an elbow over the branch, if you can," he advised. "You don't want to fall to the ground."

At length the last rope was severed: and Conan, supported by the small thief, slid limply down. Propped against the tree trunk, the injured man silently endured the torment as Subotai rubbed his bruised and sunburned limbs to restore the circulation. Proffering a leathern flask of water, he said: "Rinse your mouth out first and spit. Then take a few small sips. If you drink as much as you'd like to, it will sicken you or worse. I've seen men die that way."

"I know," grunted the Cimmerian. "Have you aught to eat?"

"First let me start a signal fire, to fetch Valeria. We've been hunting for you. A fortuneteller said that you would be south of the Mountain of Power, but he could not tell us more."

The Hyrkanian gathered twigs from the litter at the foot of the dead tree, broke off a couple of small branches, and with flint and steel soon had a brisk fire going. Then, searching the neighborhood, he discovered a few faded blades of grass that, added to the blaze, caused a billowing cloud of smoke. That done, Subotai picked up the dead vulture and, squatting down, began to pluck the bird.

"What in Crom's name are you doing?" muttered Conan.

"Taking the feathers off," replied the small thief.

"You do not mean to cook that thing!"

"Why not? Flesh is flesh, and we're both hungry."

Conan controlled his desire to retch, and grumbled: "If I am to sup, you will have to feed me. My hands are useless."

Subotai nodded and bent over his small fire. Soon pieces of broiling vulture meat impaled on a sharpened stick were merrily spattering fat into the fire, and the delicious smell of cooking filled the air. After his spare but welcome meal, Conan sighed. Then, with his back against the Tree of Woe, he fell asleep.

Conan awoke to find himself among the burial mounds of the dead kings, near the shores of the Sea of Vilayet. Valeria was bending over him, bathing and salving his wounds. He had a faint memory—or was it a dream—of sitting Valeria's horse while she rode behind him, guiding the beast, and steadying him each time he began to topple from the saddle.

He stared at his hands, stiff, swollen, and inflamed. To

move a finger was sheer agony. "Never to bear a sword again," he muttered. "I might as well be dead!"

Then consciousness again flickered out, and reality existed no more. The endless hours on the Tree of Woe had so sapped the Cimmerian's store of animal vitality that those who tended him feared that he might not recover from his wounds. He burned with a raging fever; his faith in his own strength was gone.

"Does he yet live?" inquired the old shaman, shuffling to the doorway of the hut, beyond which lay the dying man.

"Aye, but barely," replied the girl. "Old man, he called you a wizard. Have you any magic that can help him now? Or do your gods owe you a favor?"

The shaman eyed her silently. Taking his somber stare as a confession that he did indeed have otherworldly powers, Valeria cried: "Then work your spells! Put strength back into the hands that must wield the sword of vengeance!"

The old man looked weary but resigned. "For such a spell, there is a heavy price. There always is for such a rite of magic. The spirits that haunt this sacred place and guard the tombs of kings exact their toll."

"Whatever the price, I will gladly pay it!" said Valeria. "To work, sorcerer!"

A strange wind moaned, and shadows prowled amongst the tombs. Above the quicksilver surface of the Vilayet Sea, a gibbous moon showed the pallid face of a restless ghost, whose dark radiance illumined the barren earth between two of the larger monuments. In this uncouth place, while Valeria and Subotai watched with rapt attention, the shaman bound Conan's limbs with strips of sable cloth and veiled his inert body with a shroudlike material of the same funereal hue. With another strip he encircled the barbarian's head, carefully covering his bruised and sun-burned eyelids. Upon this bandage, with deft strokes of a small brush, the old man painted a row of cryptic glyphs.

The wizard next dispatched Subotai to the seashore, bidding him to fetch a bucket of clear water; and when the water was brought, the shaman squatted on a piece of carpeting to meditate and gather up his powers. Valeria,

alert to every move the old man made, sensed that he was
reaching deep into his soul to tap a dormant source of inner
strength.

Finally, the shaman roused himself from his mystic
trance. He ceremoniously sprinkled the water over all of
Conan's body, as he mumbled potent names beneath his
breath. This done, he bid the Hyrkanian bind Conan's limbs
securely to four stakes, driven deeply into the ground.

"Why so?" demanded Valeria.

Somberly, the shaman watched Subotai at work.
"During the night," he said, "the spirits of this place,
angered by my magic, will try to take the young man hence.
If they succeed . . ." His voice trailed off.

Valeria unsheathed her dagger and turned its blade
until it glinted in the moonlight. "If your spirits bear him
off, old man, you will soon follow." In the hushed
darkness, the girl's fierce words assailed the moon with all
the venom of a cornered cougar.

The shaman merely shrugged; but a faint smile, at
youthful ardor long forgotten, trembled on his lips. Slowly
the night dragged on, while the three held vigil among the
ancient tombs. The uncaring moon climbed high in the
velvet sky and picked her way among the stars. Southward,
the Mountain of Power thrust up an ominous cone, black
against the luminous darkness of the star-strewn sky. No
cricket chirped. The silence was complete.

Suddenly, Valeria gripped the Hyrkanian's wrist. Subotai, who had been dozing, swore as the girl's nails
pierced his skin. Then he, too, stared at Conan.

The huge Cimmerian's shrouded form was heaving
—moving uncannily, without volition, as if seized by giant,
invisible hands. The ropes that held him tensed and
groaned; the stakes creaked under the strain of enormous
unseen forces.

"They'll tear him apart!" wailed Valeria, as Conan's
body twitched and thrashed about so violently that one stake
was ripped from the ground. The shaman made no answer,
but he began a strange chant pitched to a silent scream and
moved his bony hands in mystical gestures.

Valeria leaped to her feet and threw herself on Conan's
body, shouting imprecations at the night. As the frantic girl

wrestled with unseen powers, snarling like a lioness protect-
ing her cub, Subotai fumbled for his scimitar. Then,
bounding forward, he slashed through the empty air above
the Cimmerian's unconscious body and the girl who strove
to weigh it down.

To Valeria's surprise, the shrouded body slumped and
lay motionless on its pallet. A wind sprang up from the sea
and shadowy presences, borne aloft like shreds of mist,
seemed to float away.

"They have gone," sighed the shaman, shivering. "My
spell was potent, and they failed." The look he cast upon
Valeria was full of pity.

As the morning sun leaped above the ocean waves, the
wizard removed the sepulchral wrappings from Conan's
body. Subotai gasped. Valeria clapped her hands to her
cheeks to curb the tears that welled up in her weary eyes.

The giant Cimmerian awoke, yawned, and stretched.
Then he studied his hands in sheer amazement. His cuts and
bruises—even the holes in his palms—had healed as if his
ordeal had never been. With a grin of delight, he held his
hands before his face, turning them to study every angle.
The wounds made by the nails had closed to small,
well-healed scars; the fingers, which had been grotesquely
swollen, were back to normal size. He clenched and
unclenched his hands to see if they still functioned.

"Wizard, I owe you a great debt," the barbarian
rumbled. Beaming, the old man nodded.

Valeria, who had pledged her life for his, and who was
wan with sleepless anxiety, tightened her encircling arms
around the Cimmerian and kissed him repeatedly, saying:
"My love is stronger than death. Neither deities nor demons
from the nether regions can separate us! If I were dead, and
you in peril, remember that I'd return from the abyss—from
the very pits of Hell—to fight by your side. . . ."

Conan grinned, and crushing her to him, kissed her
lustily. Valeria, unsatisfied still, persisted. "Promise me
that you'll remember, always."

Smiling at her womanly concern, Conan kissed her
again and said, "Don't worry; I'll remember."

XII

The Cleft

As Conan and his friends rejoiced in the wizard's humble hut, the night was filled with laughter in distant Shadizar. In the great hall of the palace, Osric, King of Zamora, made wassail. His seers had informed him that Conan had reached the Mountain of Power and penetrated the recesses of its most secret temple; now the king looked forward to the imminent return of his daughter.

His age-worn frame was decked in robes of glittering brocade, his bent fingers glowed with splendid rings; he sat on his throne proudly, sipping rich wine from a cup of beaten gold. In the cheerful light of many candles, some as tall as a five-year child and as thick as a man's thigh, lordly courtiers strolled in all their finery or gathered near the monarch to renew friendships long grown cold. At Osric's feet, slave girls in loose trousers of bright transparent gauze reclined on purple and crimson cushions, reminding those with long acquaintance of the warrior-king of bygone years, before the cult of Set had infected the land with fear and loathing.

Yet even here in the throne room itself, the king did not feel safe from the assassins of the cult leader Doom; thus, grim-faced guards stood in pairs at every portal and at each open window to secure the monarch from stealthy footsteps in the night.

Osric broke off his unwonted banter as the chief chamberlain approached the throne, candlelight flashing from the polished curves of his silver mace of office. "Sire," he said, "I desire a word with you."

The king beckoned the official to come closer. "What is it, Choros?"

"Sire, he has come again—Yaro, the black priest of Doom. He begs a private audience with Your Majesty on some high matter of state."

The king bared his teeth in a mirthless grin. "Begs, you say. Demands, like as not. Well, bid the dog back to his kennel, and leave me to my rare moment of pleasure."

"But, Sire," the chamberlain persisted, "he has imparted to me that the matter concerns your daughter, the Princess Yasimina."

The king's face turned gray; his eyes grew dull. "Very well. But have the fellow searched most thoroughly. Do not overlook his rings, brooches, or other ornaments. These snake-worshipers are cunning men and treacherous. In their hands, the most unlikely object may become a deadly weapon."

As the chamberlain bowed and withdrew, Osric beckoned to the captain of the guard.

"Clear the room. Tell my guests affairs of state press in upon me. I want no witnesses, save only Manes and Bagoas, my most trusted guards. Have each stand behind a pillar, ready to emerge in case the black dog attempts treachery."

"Aye, aye, Sire," said the captain.

"And as they go, bid the servants extinguish the larger candles. The light does hurt my eyes."

The captain bowed and turned away, repeating the royal wishes to those about the throne. Soon courtiers, guards, and slave girls bowed and withdrew, all save the two stalwart soldiers who took their stand behind a pair of massive pillars near the royal seat. As the candles were snuffed out, long shadows crawled like serpents across the marble tiles.

Osric shuddered and wet his lips. But he sat upright

still, concealing his apprehension behind a regal mien. He drained his cup of wine and tossed the goblet aside, forgetting that the servant who would have caught it had issued from the chamber. Like a gong struck by a mallet, the vessel hit the marble and, clattering, rolled to the feet of Yaro.

The black priest had entered the audience chamber on noiseless feet and now, with slow and measured tread, approached the throne. Standing impassively before the king, he folded his arms upon his breast and inclined his shaven pate in a fleeting nod. Osric regarded him silently, but there was fear and loathing in his hooded eyes.

"Sire," the priest began.

"Well?" demanded the monarch, a false bravado strengthening his quavering voice. "You desired words with me. To what import?"

"Great import, Sire," replied Yaro taking a step closer to the throne. "My Lord, Thulsa Doom, the true prophet of Set the Eternal, wishes to honor your house by marriage with your daughter, the Princess Yasimina."

"Honor my house!" cried Osric shrilly. "Honor! You abuse the word, sir, and my patience."

"Sire, marriage is an honorable estate. . . ."

"Monstrous! You have the insolence to come here and say that?" The king clawed at his beard with a shaking hand. "Your effrontery surpasses all belief!"

"No effrontery was intended," said Yaro tonelessly. "The honor that Doom would do you extends beyond yourself. It is the Grand Master's wish that, by this alliance, Zamora shall become the true kingdom of Set, and the center of an ever-expanding empire."

Quivering with fury, Osric rose. "Enough!" he cried. "Whilst I am king, I shall never sanction this monstrous union, this hellish corruption of the marriage vows. Guards!"

The two massive bodyguards stepped from the shelter of the marble columns. Yaro looked them over. In a soft, expressionless voice he said: "You promised that we should be alone, in private audience, King Osric."

The king's laugh was the bark of an angry dog. "Think you that I would trust myself alone with a human viper of the serpent cult? I have not lived this long by offering my naked heel to the fangs of a crawling snake."

Yaro bowed with mock servility. "O wise and mighty King." Then, turning to the two armed men, he said: "If I were to ask you, would you slay this infidel for our master, Thulsa Doom?"

Like men walking in a dream, the guards drew their swords and advanced on the king, who stood, trembling, on the dais of his throne. "Help! Murder! To me, loyal guards. . . ." Osric cried in vain; his feeble shouts could not penetrate the heavy doors, firmly shut at the old king's command.

As the sound of heavy blades chopping into flesh supplanted the monarch's frantic cries, Yaro turned his back and made his way down the darkened immensity of the audience chamber. The two guards wiped the blood from their blades on the dead king's robe and followed him.

By the shores of the inland sea, Conan, Valeria, and Subotai continued to enjoy the hospitality of the hermit-wizard. In the course of a few days, the Cimmerian had fully regained his former vigor; and the friends sought a plan to rescue Princess Yasimina despite the mutant soldiery and the girl's entranced fascination with the cult leader.

One dusk, as they sat around a fire in the sorcerer's hut, Conan said, "The old man tells me that the Mountain of Power contains a vast network of chambers, some natural caves and others hollowed out by those who built Doom's templed hiding place. I saw some of those chambers when I went thither in the guise of a pilgrim."

Valeria said: "You tried to enter by the door open to the faithful, and you nearly died of it. If we dare not try that way again, how shall we enter?"

"There is a secret entrance," muttered Conan. "Behind the mountain, a stream has cut a deep and narrow gorge. Far up the gorge, there is an unguarded opening. The old man says none knows of it but he."

"You mean," said Subotai, "that a good thief could climb the gorge, steal the girl, and be off before anyone would miss her?"

"How does the wizard know about this opening?" Valeria asked suspiciously.

"The ancient sorcerer has lived his life in these parts," rumbled Conan. "He prowled the mountain passages before Doom came to this land."

Subotai, picking his teeth with a splinter, added, "From whatever pit of Hell it was that spawned him!"

"That same Hell to which, Crom grant, I shall return him!" The Cimmerian's angry eyes glowed a volcanic blue, and his right hand clenched as if around the pommel of a sword.

Valeria looked sharply at Conan. Unable to read his saturnine expression, she said, "We have come here for one purpose only—to fetch the girl Yasimina to her father and to gain a kingly fortune. Later there will be time to seek revenge; later, when we have Osric's promised treasure, we can hire assassins or raise whole armies to lay siege to yonder fortress."

Subotai nodded his agreement. Conan sat silently caressing with his thumb the edge of his sturdy weapon. Valeria said no more.

In the chill of the following dawn, they parted from the wizard. The wind ruffled the manes of the three horses as Valeria galloped off, her blonde hair floating behind her on a freshet of moving air. Subotai paused to adjust his bow and quiver full of well-tipped arrows before he followed her. Keeping a tight rein on his gelding, Conan trotted over to the sorcerer, who sat glumly on the threshold of his now empty abode.

The wizard, lost in prayers or contemplation, rubbed one gnarled hand upon the other, seemingly unaware of the Cimmerian's approach. His eyes remained averted, even when the other spoke.

"Wish us well, old man," said the barbarian, "for today we lie on the laps of the careless gods."

Not certain that his words had been received, Conan waved a salute to the bent and indrawn figure, wheeled his steed, and galloped off to join the others. With tears streaming down his weathered cheeks, the wise man gazed after him until horse and rider were swallowed in mists from the Vilayet Sea.

The three adventurers crossed the plain and, choosing an obscure path, skirted the flanks of the Mountain of Power with care, lest they be noticed by sentries posted on the heights. In time, they entered a region of broken foothills, through which a stream had chiseled a deep cleft. Ahead, this channel rose steeply to a tremendous height. Hemmed in by these sheer walls of stone, a spring-fed stream tumbled and casacaded down the mountain side, rushed, seething, over boulders and pebbled sands, to swirl at last into quiet pools among the rock slides.

Here, where dwarfed trees clung to the sparse soil, the three dismounted and tethered their horses. Subotai drew from his saddle bags several curious objects, which he had constructed with the shaman's help. These were goatskin bags, their seams caulked with pitch. While the two men inflated these grotesque spheres, tying the necks tightly, Valeria combined in a small bowl mineral oil and powdered charcoal to make a thick and sticky pigment. Setting aside their outer garments, they smeared their bodies with a mottled pattern, resembling sunlight dancing on long shadows. Black bands confined their hair; and in these sable strips they placed small branches of leafy greens, so that the casual observer would see a bush, and not a human form.

In the gray light of a sunless afternoon, the rushing torrent looked icy cold and perilous, but there was no other way to steal into the citadel. So, tying favorite weapons, wrapped in dark cloth, to their backs, and clasping the inflated bags of hide, one by one they abandoned themselves to the stream.

Sometimes breasting the freezing water, sometimes clambering upward on submerged rocks, they clawed their way to the margin of the flume. There, where the water fell with brutal force, Conan seized an upthrust spire and clambered to the top of a steep bank. Soon Valeria and Subotai followed him from the water; and, their bodies atingle from the cold kiss of the wind, they began to work their way up the crude staircase formed by forbidding rocks.

Beside them the falling water roared like thunder; above them the cliff walls seemed to intersect, shuttering out the pale light of fading day. They paused to rest where a particularly large boulder offered a moment's refuge. Looking up they saw, high on the massive cliffs, the glow of fire framed by the entrance to a cave. The opening was a mere cleft in the rock wall, tall and narrow, like the pointed window of a fortress.

Suddenly, above the thunder of the waterfall, they heard the slow and measured cadence of beaten drums. As they resumed their tortuous climb, the low and resonant throbbing increased in volume, deep-throated, persistent, unrelenting. Conan whispered to the girl behind him: "Sounds as if the devil Doom is about to greet his benighted fools. If only I could get my hands on him . . ."

Valeria felt panic freeze her heart, panic far colder than the chill wind on her naked back. It lent an urgency to her half-audible reply. "Just the girl, Conan. We came for just the girl."

The Cimmerian nodded briefly and continued on his upward climb. Shadowlike in the dusk, they reached the entrance to the cave and wriggled through. As silently as wraiths cavorting in a graveyard, Conan and Valeria wedged themselves into small fissures in the cave walls, while Subotai, on stealthy feet, moved forward toward the firelight.

The drums fell silent; and hiding in the dark recesses, the invaders heard a cacophony of little sounds: a squeaking that might have been the voices of hungry rats; the slow drip of water on stone; and, from the cave entrance, a weird ululation of the wind.

At length Subotai returned from his explorations and signaled them excitedly. They inched their way forward, trying not to dislodge a wayward pebble, lest the slipping stone betray them.

"Hark!" growled Conan, stopping suddenly. "The drums again. . . ." In some chamber set above the rocky ceiling of the narrow cave, they heard the maniacal fury of the drums, loud and demanding, and with the pounding noise, a plaintive chanting from a hundred youthful voices tuned to the frenzied beat. Under the cover of this all-encompassing noise, the three made their way to the larger cave wherein lay the source of the firelight.

Before them, lit by many bonfires, was a scene from Hell itself. The leaping flames painted the rocky roof far above their heads yellow, and orange, and red; and by this unearthly illumination, they discovered the immensity of the cavern that opened out before them. Vast it was as the interior of a temple; and, like a place of worship, the dome-shaped roof was supported by a series of limestone columns. These, however, seemed not to be the work of man, but rather the result of dripping water divesting itself of bits of lime over untold centuries. Wonder vied with caution as they beheld this natural magnificence.

"Guards!" hissed Subotai, touching Conan's arm; for suddenly, in the flickering firelight, the intruders saw the moving forms of armed men. At Conan's gesture, they glided back into the shadows and sought places of concealment. There, in the dappled darkness, their mottled bodies invisible, they prepared for action. The Hyrkanian drew his bow from its case, and, setting an end on the stone flooring, strung the weapon with a practiced motion. Conan loosened his sword from its cloth-wrapped scabbard, while Valeria unsheathed her long knife. Soon, they knew, they would need all their skill at arms.

XIII

The Cavern

From his place of concealment, Conan peered warily at the leaping flames and the burly guards in iron and leather. He licked his lips, but otherwise stood motionless, as if awaiting some signal that would launch him into battle with these brutes; for there appeared to be no way to gain entry to the cavern except by force.

Subotai seemed unhappy. A thief rejoices in his mastery of the furtive arts, and a straightforward fight tests none of the larcenous skills on which he prides himself. At length, he whispered: "Must we fight our way in, Cimmerian? I'm no coward, Erlik knows; but it seems folly to seek our goal against such odds, when by craft and stealth we could gain our ends unscathed."

Valeria nodded. "They have their backs to us. That gives us some advantage."

Conan grunted assent. "They know nothing of the entrance from the gorge—if the old wizard spoke true."

"He's been right so far," murmured Valeria.

Conan growled something inarticulate. The young Cimmerian was spoiling for a fight. His blood was up, and he yearned to repay his enemies for the sufferings they had inflicted on him. Still, he realized that to reveal their presence so early would lose them the advantage of surprise.

Subotai, whose darting glances had been studying their surroundings, whispered excitedly: "Look over there, to the left! See you those clusters of rock columns free-standing from the cavern wall? They'll make a screen for us if we can scramble along the cave side without making too much noise."

"It is narrow," objected Valeria, "and the wall juts out in places. You and I might get through, but what of Conan?"

Conan grinned. "I don't mind leaving a little skin behind, if I must," he grunted. "I'd get rid of this oily muck on my hide, at least."

Led by Subotai, they threaded their way along the cavern wall, their progress curtained by the stalagmites that rose like giant's teeth from the bedrock. Their rude path led upward, so that, when they paused to survey the scene from a break in the rocky curtain, they found themselves looking down across the whole immensity of the cavern floor.

They saw in the center a huge cauldron upheld by four massive posts of blackened stone, the vessel itself of some substance that, from the distance, looked like stone. Flames roared up from firepits cut out of the rocky floor, the leaping blaze clawing the smoky air.

All around the cauldron, huge, sweat-covered beast-men worked to feed the flames beneath the vast cook pot, while other hairy workers struggled with some contraption that stirred the steaming contents. Great chunks of boiling meat floated in the bubbling bowl, while apelike butchers cut up other carcasses to add to the aromatic stew. Beyond the cook pot stretched a generous dining hall furnished with trestle tables and benches made of logs.

Suddenly the three intruders stiffened and stared in disbelief. Hung from meat hooks to one side of the great cauldron, half-hidden by the steam and the flickering firelight, they saw human bodies, drawn and bloodless, like those of beef sides or plucked fowl. From the delicate, almost translucent flesh that covered the pallid faces and immobile limbs, it was clear that the victims had once been pilgrims to the Mountain of Power, followers of the serpent

god. As the three adventurers watched in horror, a pair of
beast-men hacked up one body with their cleavers and,
trotting over to the cauldron, tossed the pieces into the
boiling liquid.

Valeria turned pale, and buried her face against Conan's shoulder. The Cimmerian swore an oath beneath his
breath. Subotai retched. Fortunately, the rhythmic beating
of the drums increased in volume and masked the telltale
sound. As the noise swelled, the watchers' attention focused on the frenzied beating, which filled the cavern with
reverberating echoes. The drums were as huge as the
cauldron; the taut hide stretched across each top was set to
vibrating, not by hands or drumsticks, but by the bare feet
of grotesque, capering figures.

The dancing figures, either naturally as hirsute as
beasts or wrapped closely in the skins of wild animals,
seemed oddly deformed. The shadows they cast in the
uncertain light of the flames wore the shape of fiends from
the nethermost reaches of Hell.

"What manner of man or devil are they?" whispered
Subotai, incredulously.

Conan shrugged, remembering the hulking, anthropoid
guards whom he had passed on his way into the temple.

The whispers of the raiders were silenced by the clank
of armor. They shrank back into deeper gloom, as a squad
of hairy men in metal-mounted leather marched into the
dining hall, tugged off their helmets, and settled down to
feed. Soon they were joined by a straggle of latecomers,
whose noisy gruntings added to the din.

Conan jerked a peremptory thumb to urge his companions on. Proceeding with utmost caution, they circled past
the seething cauldron with its ghastly contents, and in time
came to another section of the cavern used as a dwelling
place by the cave folk. Here the women and children of the
troglodytes, as ugly as the males, pursued their domestic
affairs.

"Trolls!" muttered Subotai, his eyes widening. "The
legends of my people tell of them."

Valeria shook her head. "No, they are the descendents
of an ancient race, who dwelt in caves from times beyond
man's memory."

"How could they thus have sunk to the level of beasts?" muttered the small Hyrkanian.

Valeria said: "From what I have heard, such is not the case. They are not men who have become animals, but animals who have almost grown to men. My people say that long, long ago there were two branches of man: our forebears and these shadow-dwellers. My ancestors called them that because these beast-men could not endure the light of day and chose to make their home in the hollows beneath the earth. When our forebears spread out across the land, seeking the daylight and the fertile earth, these shadow-dwellers burrowed ever deeper into the ground."

"And fed on human flesh," added Subotai disgustedly.

Valeria nodded. "This Doom must breed them here for his unholy purposes. He feeds them on the bodies of his cult-worshipers. Or on those he teaches his followers to kill."

Conan glowered. "That's how the snake prophet protects his mindless children—with an army of cannibal beast-men whose bellies are filled with the fools who follow him."

"Or those who wish to follow him no more," said Subotai.

Beyond the living quarters of the cave folk, the three raiders reached the far end of the great cavern, and found themselves confronted by a bridge of thong-bound poles suspended between two mammoth logs. This narrow bridge spanned a wide, deep fissure, which had been opened up in eons past by some violent convulsion within the mountain. Beyond this obstacle they perceived a generous, man-made portal through which shone a strange, opalescent light. Seeing no guard about, they ventured into the open, with Subotai, arrow nocked, in the lead.

Suddenly, at the far end of the bridge, an apelike boy appeared. About four feet tall, the beast-child was already of a muscular, stocky build that bespoke enormous strength. Pulling a hatchet from his girdle, he snarled and gesticulated wildly. Then he charged.

"They can't talk," rumbled Conan, preparing to defend himself and the girl behind him.

Even as the Cimmerian spoke, a bowstring twanged; and the boy stood transfixed by an arrow. He shrieked, staggered, and tumbled into the chasm.

Subotai sighed. "He was only a boy."

"Yes, but he would have grown up," said Valeria. "Let's move on."

Led by the incandescent greenish glow, they hastened through the unguarded portal and found themselves in a narrow hallway, such as servants use when attending to the orders of their masters. There was no sign of any who might challenge them; yet they moved on furtive feet, hugging the wall to take advantage of every shadow.

"This must be the entrance for the guards of Thulsa Doom," muttered Conan, "and of those who serve the faithful followers of Set."

Subotai nodded. "And since they are all servants of the snake-god, Doom feels no need to post a sentinel here."

"Let's still go with caution," said Valeria. "We do not know what awaits us further on."

Stealthily they proceeded along the hall and up a rock-hewn stairway; and much amazed, they found themselves at the threshold of a chamber draped in filmy gauze to form, as it were, a pavilion through which the green light pulsed. Around it, half-hidden by the translucent curtains, as by an evening mist, the astonished intruders saw graceful trees and beds of delicate-hued flowers, planted in soil-filled hollows to re-create a garden within the confines of the cave. The floor of polished blue-black marble gleamed like the still waters of a lake, and from silver vessels incense curled upward through the motionless air. Above the distant throbbing of the drums, a flute sang like a nightingale to weave a sense-seducing spell.

Into the ethereal glow of this fairyland crept the three raiders, gliding like insubstantial shadows from shrub to shrub. Behind the draperies of the pavilion they perceived dozens of young people of both sexes clad in gossamer or not at all. Some lay in slumber; others languidly made love; yet others sat in a deathlike trance, their backs propped up against the slender columns of malachite, which upheld the draperies that formed the place of pleasure.

So slowly did the pleasure-seekers move, if indeed they moved at all, that Conan looked at his companions and wordlessly formed the word, "Drugged!"

Subotai's quick glance picked out one guard and then another, their anthropoid, hairy bodies stretched out in swinish sleep beside those whose guardians they were. Even the leopards, chained to a column, had been affected by the potent narcotic that wafted upward with the incense; for they had laid their slumberous heads between their paws and closed their eyes of molten gold.

Suddenly, Valeria touched Conan's arm and pointed. With a shock, Conan recognized his ancient enemy. Thulsa Doom sat in an alcove, in a trancelike state, his legs and arms crossed, his head bowed, the better to inhale a spiral of drugged vapor that rose from a carven bowl placed on a brazier.

Before him knelt Princess Yasimina of Shadizar. Her transparent garment had fallen from her shoulders, exposing the gentle swell of her high breasts. While two handmaidens chanted an exotic paean in a strange language, the princess—like one sunk in a sensual dream—slowly undulated her naked torso and ran eager hands up and down her bare thighs. Her head was thrown back, her eyes half-closed, and she licked her lips with the tip of her tongue.

Lethargically, Doom raised his head and feasted his eyes on the girl's exposed beauty.

"The princess?" whispered Valeria. Conan nodded. His blue eyes blazed with anger and disgust.

"So this is the Paradise of Set!" murmured Subotai. "The prophet might convert me from the worship of Erlik, if the women were as wakeful as they are willing."

Valeria eyed him coldly. Then turning to Conan, she breathed, "What now?" But he made no answer.

"If we wait a while," Subotai replied, "they will all fall asleep. And then . . . What say you, Cimmerian?"

Two pairs of eyes sought Conan's face; but his attention was riveted to the wall of the alcove wherein Doom and Yasimina were lost in their narcotic dreams. Valeria gasped. Never had she seen such an expression on Conan's face. Hate and animal ferocity possessed the

Cimmerian's countenance, and with it a heart-aching sadness that lay too deep for tears.

Valeria and Subotai directed a questing glance at the jade-green wall behind the cult leader and his priestess. There, supported by two silver pegs, hung a heavy broadsword, the crossguard fashioned in the form of a stag's antlers, and the pommel shaped like the hooves of elk. Long and superbly crafted was the blade, and its polished length flashed like a mirror in the dim green light.

It was a work of art, a weapon of pure Atlantean steel —the sword forged by Conan's father.

XIV

The Rescue

Oblivious to the scene before him, the young Cimmerian, casting caution to the winds of fate, stepped forward. To regain his father's sword alone possessed him. Valeria and Subotai, with total disregard of danger, loyally moved forward at his side.

As the three figures, arms at the ready, cut off all escape from the alcove, Thulsa Doom strove to cast off the stupor that held him in thrall. His eyes narrowed as he focused on the three determined faces and the three blades no more than a few strides from his person. An anger more terrible than any the two Pit fighters had ever seen twisted his visage and for a moment immobilized them.

Valeria sank the nails of her left hand into Conan's sword arm and whispered, "Look!"

Subotai drew in his breath and swore a Hyrkanian oath. One of the leopards chained to a pillar opened its golden cat's eyes and, with twitching ears, watched silently. Conan stared.

A weird change was coming over the slender form of Doom. His neck rippled and seemed to lengthen. The lower part of his face bulged forward, elongating his jaws. His aquiline nose shriveled and disappeared as his forehead receded. Cracks appeared on his ascetic face, narrow dark lines like those on river ice during a spring thaw. The cracks connected and formed a pattern of huge, overlapping scales. As his lips thinned and vanished, his sleepy eyes rounded into lidless orbs with slit pupils ringed in red. A forked tongue of dark purple flicked out of the serpent's head that Doom now wore, wavered to test the air, and speedily withdrew

"Crom!" muttered Conan, as the serpent head and neck swayed, as a cobra sways in its basket to the whine of the snake-charmer's pipe or the motion of his body.

Subotai was the first to recover his voice. "We must burn out this snake's nest!" he whispered.

Conan nodded. "Foulness like this can only be cleansed with the torch."

"But only after we get the princess," breathed Valeria. "And my father's blade."

With the speed of a pouncing puma, the Cimmerian leaped into the alcove, darted past the swaying serpent's head, and lifted the great weapon from its pegs. At the same instant, Valeria bounded across the marble floor to stand, with legs widespread and sword in hand, above the kneeling follower of Set.

"Come," she whispered.

Princess Yasimina looked up at the warrior woman, magnificent in her strength and determination, and screamed.

"Get up," Valeria commanded; and when the terrified girl failed to obey, she seized her long hair and pulled her to her feet.

Feebly, the stupefied girl struggled as Valeria grasped her arm and half-dragged her, whimpering, across the room in which the sated lovers and drugged celebrants lay with their guards in passionless self-absorption.

Once the unwilling princess had left the alcove, Conan and Subotai snatched up candles and touched the flaming tapers to the drifting curtains that framed the resting place of Thulsa Doom. The handmaidens, aroused by the acrid stench of burning cloth, fled to the central pavilion, but they found no refuge there.

Covering Valeria's retreat, Conan and Subotai paused only long enough to touch a candle flame to one gauze drapery, then another, and another. One by one the cultists woke, coughing and rubbing smoke-filled eyes. Then, seeing blazing curtains all around them, they shrieked in mindless terror and scrambled for exits at the far end of the chamber.

One brutish guard interposed himself between the raiders and the stairway by which they sought to flee. Suddenly, there was a flash of steel; and the beast-man fell, half hacked in two by Conan's Atlantean steel. Subotai thrust a lighted taper into the face of a turbaned youth who came at him with a dagger. Screaming and clutching his singed forehead, the boy staggered off.

As he neared the sheltering stairs, the Cimmerian glanced back, searching the incandescent room for Thulsa Doom, hoping to find him lying dead in his alcove. But even as he looked, his hope was dashed. The curtains no longer smoldered; the smoke had rolled away; and there was no trace of the wizard, who seemed none other than the serpent-god himself.

Beyond the chaos, near to the narrow stairs up which the invaders had come, stood Valeria. At her feet crouched a distraught and trembling Yasimina, whose furtive glances bespoke a frantic search for an opportunity to escape her captor.

Suddenly, a tight little smile flitted across her sullen lips. Like a firefly, it lit her face for a brief moment and vanished; to Valeria, with her training as a Pit fighter, it flashed a message of trouble to come. She heard a scrape of boots on the stairs, faint as the sound was above the throb of the incessant drums in the cavern below and the screams of panic in the once lovely fairyland created for lovers and their beloved. Valeria whirled.

With her blade flashing like a serpent's tongue, she faced an enormous warrior clad in iron-studded leather. Although he was not young, his face was as grim as death, and the muscles of his sword arm looked as strong as bands of steel. He was flanked by four hairy guards, carrying spiked wooden clubs, and menace glowed in their bestial eyes.

"Rexor!" trilled Princess Yasimina. "Rexor, save me! Save me for our Master who loves me!"

Kneeing the princess to the floor, Valeria crouched to avoid a blow from a guardsman's mace. Then, with lightning speed, she sprang. Her tulwar licked out, and death was on its point. The guard staggered and clutched his throat, whence blood spurted out between his hairy fingers.

Leaping, twisting, dodging, Valeria circled the guards, avoiding blows of the maces that would have smashed her like an insect. A second guard lumbered forward, snarling and growling, but the lithe girl feinted and thrust into the opening between the leathern plates of the brute's armor. The anthropoid grunted, clutched his torn belly, and then collapsed. Her blade, now crimson-stained, caught another in the neck. Shrieking horribly, he rushed forward. Valeria jumped aside, allowing the momentum of his forward thrust to carry him into a burning drapery in the center of the room.

Then Rexor and the remaining guard closed in on her. As they backed her into a corner, she knew that she was boxed in and soon would be denied the speed that was the basis of her successes. Just then Conan, like a stalking jungle beast, glided between two blazing draperies, his father's great sword held in two bronze fists. The beast-man turned at the Cimmerian's approach, but Conan's heavy sword sheared through his armor and dropped him to his knees with a split skull.

As Valeria moved toward Doom's first lieutenant, Conan roared: "There goes the princess! Catch her! Leave Rexor to me!"

The giant's eyes flashed red at the sight of the young Cimmerian. He had left Conan broken and hung on the Tree of Woe; now he was whole and hale. But Rexor had no time to ponder the miracle; the great sword clenched in Conan's hands was upraised in preparation for a mighty downstroke.

Two blades clashed together with the fury of a tempest. A shower of sparks signaled a ringing crash as Rexor's weapon, responding to the impact of Atlantean steel on lesser iron, clattered on the marble floor. Rexor hurled his hilt at Conan's head; and, as the Cimmerian ducked, the cultist warrior sprang forward and wrapped unrelenting arms around his huge antagonist.

Conan dropped his father's sword, for it was useless at such close quarters, and met his opponent's wrestling grip with undiminished strength. The two giants staggered about the burning room, unmindful of the smoke and flames, their powerful thews swelling as they matched two wills of iron. Relentlessly, they clawed and gouged and kicked at one another. When at last Rexor gripped Conan's throat, his massive fingers bit like the jaws of a steel trap into the Cimmerian's corded neck. Conan, fighting for life-giving air, managed to pry one gross finger loose and bent it back until the bone cracked. With a howl of pain and fury, Rexor released his grasp and hurled the younger man against the central pillar.

While Conan, half stunned, sagged against the malachite column, struggling to gather his wits, Rexor stooped for the great sword forged by the Cimmerian's father so long ago. Just then one of the leopards, maddened by the fire and smoke, snapped the chain that bound it to the pillar, pounced on Rexor's back, and bore him to the ground. The stricken man fought in vain against the sharp claws of the animal. At length, he fell screaming to the pave, while the frantic cat leaped away, its broken chain clattering along the marble tiles as it made its way to safety.

Conan, head spinning, got to his feet. Rexor lay sprawled in a pool of blood, the great sword beyond his convulsive grasp. Recovering the weapon, the Cimmerian youth searched through the pervasive smoke for Valeria and the princess. He saw the girl-thief back among the charred draperies striving to control their unwilling captive.

As he started forward, an ominous creaking above his head caused Conan to glance up. The supports of the pavilion, along which little flames ran like luminous mice, had begun to crumble; one beam, then another, fell. The stone column upon which the roof pole rested cracked, spilling broken bits of stone across the polished floor.

Pausing no longer, the barbarian rushed to Valeria's aid. Yasimina was struggling to flee and, despite her skill and determination, Valeria's strength was fading. As Conan reached his exhausted comrade-in-arms, the roar of collapsing masonry resounded through the fast-emptying chamber. The malachite pillar gave way and toppled, pinning Rexor to the ground, while crumpled tent cloth, half-burned beams, and broken roof tiles nearly entombed the fallen man.

The spectacular collapse of the fantastic setting and the prolonged rumble of its destruction distracted Valeria; and, in that single moment, Yasimina wrenched her arms free and sped away. The Cimmerian sprang after her. In a few long strides, he caught up with her and whirled her around.

The besotted girl, screeching imprecations, clawed at Conan's face.

Aware of the danger to the princess as well as to her rescuers should more guards arrive, Conan abandoned his code of barbaric chivalry and slapped her hard across her face. Amazed, the hysterical girl fell silent, offering no further resistance as he scooped up her slender body, tossed it over one brawny shoulder, and ran for the exit, with Valeria at his heels.

They zigzagged through the chamber, dodging piles of smoldering rubble and terrified groups of the faithful, who belatedly sought their way through the smoke to the safety of their leader's inner corridors. Near the stairs up which they had come, Conan and Valeria found Subotai crouched behind an urn, an arrow at the ready lest other anthropoid guards should seek entry to the burning ruin, which had once been a pleasure garden in a vaulted cave.

As his companions emerged from the acrid haze, Subotai shouted, "This way, ere the fire spreads and cuts us off!"

Bounding down the narrow stairs, they returned to the huge cavern wherein dwelt the families of the apelike servitors of Thulsa Doom. They hurried across the bridge just in time to hide behind a boulder when a contingent of the guard clattered past on their way to fight the fire. Melting into the gloom, Valeria and Subotai led the Cimmerian and his unconscious burden along the narrow passage among the enshrouding rocks towards the cleft through which they had made their entrance. And all the while, the great drums beat out their frenzied chant of "Doom! Doom! Doom!"

Behind them, where once had stood the pavilion of pleasure, the fire and chaos subsided. The singed and wearied fire fighters fell back and stood with bowed and humble heads as Thulsa Doom strode from the inner reaches of his fortress mountain, his body clad in armor, his head returned to mortal guise, his eyes blazing with fury. The leader of the beast-guard stepped forward to salute him.

"Thank Set you live, Master!" he cried. "We knew our god would keep you safe from harm!"

The cult leader nodded briefly, then anger suffused his

slit-eyed, pallid face. "Where is the priestess Yasimina? Why is she not here to welcome me?"

A heap of rubble moved; a groan issued forth. At Doom's command, the guards lifted up charred timbers and tore away the smoldering remains of once-lovely furnishings. Willing hands helped Rexor to rise. Bloody and battered, he stood before the leader of the cult.

Doom's wrath flared. "Know you where is the princess?"

"The man you crucified and others—they killed three guards; they cut me; they carried her off while I was helpless!"

"Infidels! Assassins! Purveyors of death!" the cult leader hissed. "They have violated my sanctum; they have defiled our holy place. They shall die in lakes of blood! Seek them out, good Rexor, and bring them to me, alive or dead! Go."

Rexor saluted and turned away. Followed by his lumbering beast-men, he vanished among the curls of smoke that rose above the dying coals.

Through the great cavern the invaders fled, their footsteps muffled by the beating of the incessant drums. They did not pause to watch the bubbling cauldron with its grisly contents. They did not notice the beast-men feasting in the firelight. They prayed to their separate gods that the stalagmites which sheltered them would save them from the casual glance of some sated dweller of the cave.

Then, like a miracle, a patch of starlit sky swam into view. Conan grunted with relief as they squeezed through the cleft and found themselves on the selfsame ledge from which they had breached the Mountain of Power. The same waterfall thundered nearby, a welcome change from the pounding drumbeats within the cavern.

XV

The Parting

The clean night air caressed the bruised and weary bodies of both rescuers and rescued. A faint breeze toyed with the long hair of Princess Yasimina like the fingers of a lover, and the girl stirred on the Cimmerian's broad shoulder.

"With a little luck," panted Subotai, "we can be away from this accursed place before they discover us."

Valeria whispered, "I think they missed us in the dark and are searching some other passage."

Grimly, Conan shook his sable mane. "I hear their armor rattling in the cavern. We must hurry."

He shifted Yasimina's inert form so that she lay across his back with her arms falling over his shoulders. "Tie her wrists together, Valeria. I'll need both of my hands to clamber down the rocks."

The girl-thief undid her girdle and bound the fabric around the limp wrists of the princess, muttering the while, "If the wench slips down your back, she'll strangle you."

Conan grinned. "I'll save that privilege, girl, for you alone." And, with shoulders hunched, he grasped the rocky pinnacle and felt for the nearest boulder on the rude stairs that led to safety.

As the barbarian started his cautious descent, full

consciousness returned to Yasimina. Her drug-induced dreams faded, to be replaced by a nightmare of reality. A torrent of falling water seemed about to engulf her. A bottomless black chasm yawned below, and she was being propelled into it on the greasy, ill-smelling back of a giant. Above her, silhouetted on the ledge, stood a man with arrow nocked in a taut bowstring and a woman warrior with a dirk gripped in her hand.

Yasimina screamed, and her sharp scream tore the tapestry of night.

Conan rumbled a curse on Osric and all his household, adding savagely, "Be still, unless you want to die."

But the princess, more in terror than defiance, cried hysterically: "Master, Master, save me! Lord Doom, save me!"

Conan, balancing himself precariously on a small rectangle of rock, released one handhold long enough to slap the face that nestled against his neck. Stunned, the girl fell silent. But too late.

Sentry fires on the top of the mountain began to glow. Faces peered into the dark void. Missiles whispered past him and clattered on the rocks below; whether they were weapons or mere stones, he could not tell. One glanced from his shoulder, forcing a grunt of pain through his clenched teeth. Thus, urged to greater speed by necessity, Conan completed his descent and, taking shelter behind a stunted tree, ventured to look up in search of his companions.

Valeria, as agile as a mountain goat, was working her way down the rocky stairs. Subotai, still on the ledge, was taking aim at some object high above him on the mountain. As Conan watched, an arrow winged upward, arced, and struck. With a hideous howl, a beast-man tottered and then fell, thrashing, into his signal fire.

Another arrow sped along the pathway of the first. Another guard, pierced in the chest, staggered on the brink of the precipice. He fell, shrieking, into the gorge, hurtled down the narrow throat of stone, and plunged into the waterfall before the echo of his cries ceased to reverberate.

Even as Conan watched, the first beast-men to discover the cleft began to squeeze through the slender opening.

Distracted by the eerie sound of echoing cries, they hesitated on the ledge to make dull-witted inquiry into the source of the bizarre and hollow sound. That hesitation provided Subotai the moment he needed to swing over the ledge and crouch on the stairlike rocks. Then, as they returned to the cavern to report the strange happening, the Hyrkanian clambered down the boulders and joined his fellows where the land rolled out more gently.

"Erlik boil them all in oil!" muttered Subotai, as he inspected his scraped knuckles and raw palms. "That time, I thought it was the end of me."

"Let's find the horses before the devils sound the alarm," said Valeria. "We crossed the stream somewhere hereabouts."

They strove to pierce the darkness and discover the air-filled skins on which they had crossed the fast-moving water; but the wilderness of jagged rocks and boulders was full of nooks and crannies, whose dark recesses the starlight could not penetrate. At length they abandoned the fruitless search.

"Let's follow along this bank until we reach the flatlands," said Conan, picking up Yasimina and slinging her over his left shoulder once again.

"But the stream grows wider there, and we desert men are little used to swimming," objected the Hyrkanian.

"Well, do the best you can," snapped Valeria. "We'll have our hands full with that stupid girl."

With Subotai in the lead, the three adventurers picked their way along the unfamiliar bank of the precipitous stream. They walked in silence, thankful for the cover of the moonless night and grateful that they had eluded Doom and his apelike sentinels. The burden in Conan's arms slowed their progress, but at least the sleeping princess would not summon another contingent of the guard.

Too soon, it seemed, the light of dawn suffused the sky, driving away the friendly stars. Nesting birds rose squawking above the foliage that masked their path, revealing to any who might look their whereabouts. Valeria, bringing up the rear, became apprehensive.

"I see a roadway or a path circling round the mountainside," she murmured. "What purpose do you think it serves?"

"It leads to a lookout platform for the guards, I have no doubt," rumbled the Cimmerian. "They had sentries all along the way when I made the climb along with the pilgrim sheep."

No sentries are about this morn," said Subotai cheerfully. "We're near the horses now, once we get across this millpond. The water's so calm that even I can paddle my way across."

"I'll help Conan with the pitch-haired wench." Valeria waded into the pool, shattering the surface like a broken mirror.

"Pray Crom she doesn't screech again," muttered the barbarian as he placed the princess on the supporting arms of his companion. When the cold water wakened her, Conan glared at Yasimina and growled: "Say just one word, and I'll drown you here myself."

Together Valeria and Conan towed the whimpering princess across the still water. Subotai meanwhile had splashed his way across and emerged on the grassy bank to stand guard as Conan and Valeria dragged the terror-stricken girl away from the water's edge and then threw themselves, panting, face-down on a grassy knoll.

With his thief's unceasing vigilance, Subotai's eyes patrolled the mountain path that led to the look-out platform. "Let's go, Conan, ere they sniff us out—oh, Erlik! Look you yonder!"

He pointed to the sinuous trail on the hillside above them, whereon appeared a group of marching figures.

"By Crom, it's Doom and Rexor with a squad of their subhumans," muttered Conan.

"They've discovered us," breathed Valeria. "Doom's pointing us out."

Rexor appeared to give orders; the beast-men nodded in agreement. Soon they began to scramble down the pathless waste, howling as they came. Although no spark of intelligence gleamed from their piglike eyes, their hairy arms were huge as they closed in, waving upraised weapons —clubs, maces, and sharpened axes. The sun's first rays lit up their slavering jaws and bounced off the metal studding on their leathern armor.

The three companions took their battle stance, with Valeria guarding Conan's back, while Subotai, whipping out his light tulwar, shielded Conan's left. And then the brutes were upon them. Working together, they ducked, twisted, slashed, and thrust. Each parried blows aimed at one of the others, like a flawless fighting team. Moved by love and desperation, in the ecstasy of combat, Conan and Valeria fought more skillfully than they had ever fought before, or ever would again.

Bones cracked under Conan's sledge-hammer blows. Blood flowed at the touch of Valeria's darting sword. A beast-man fell; then another and another. One seized Subotai's tulwar with a bare hand. Ignoring the pain as the razor-sharp edge sheared through skin and tendons, the creature tore the slender scimitar from the Hyrkanian's grasp, then raised his axe for the kill. As Subotai leaped back, cursing, Conan laid open the beast-man's belly.

With his back against a boulder, Subotai reached around for his bow, nocked an arrow, and released. Although the bowstring was wet and the arrow's flight unsteady, another attacker staggered off, clutching a shaft half-buried in his flesh. As suddenly as it began, the fight was over. Growling, the remaining brutes shuffled off. Like whipped dogs, they made their dispirited way up the hill to the look-out post where still stood the cult leader and his henchman.

Three pairs of weary eyes followed the guards' flight up the rough terrain. Three pairs of eyes lifted to see the regal figure of Thulsa Doom standing, legs wide-spread, attended by his first lieutenant. With lightning speed, Doom grasped a serpent, which was coiled about his neck; and, with a twisting motion, he stretched the viper out into a scale-covered arrow. Then, receiving a strung bow from Rexor's attentive hand, he drew the shaft, which but a moment sooner had been a living snake, and shot.

Straight for Conan's heart the envenomed arrow sped. Swifter still was the leap of the warrior woman, as she made herself a living shield to protect the man she loved. Thus the death-dealing arrow tip entered Valeria's breast and came to rest protruding between her slender shoulder blades.

As Valeria crumpled, Conan caught her; and, falling to his knees, he cradled her in his powerful arms. Then he looked up and glared with hate-filled eyes at his life-long enemy. Doom stood watching his lieutenant unstring the great bow. A thin and evil smile spread across his cruel face.

Rexor grinned his admiration. He shouted, "Your shot was straight and true, Master. Death to the infidel!"

The thin smile turned into an inhuman grimace. Across the open space his answer carried, "Death to all who stand against me!"

Turning on his heel, Doom walked away.

Conan bent over the wounded girl and kissed her pale lips. Then he saw the arrow point protruding from her back and pulled it through, as Valeria, too weak to cry out, gasped in pain. In the barbarian's hand, the missile became a snake again. Overcome with revulsion, he hurled it into the crystal waters of the somnolent stream.

"Live! You must live," he whispered. "I need you."

Valeria managed a wan flicker of a smile.

"The wizard . . . told me . . . that I must pay the gods. . . ." Valeria's voice was as faint as the rustle of leaves in a dying breeze. "Now I have . . . paid."

Conan held her against his breast, and their wet hair mingled blonde beneath black in the golden light of the rising sun. A wind sprang up from the Vilayet Sea.

"Hold me tight . . . tighter," moaned Valeria. "Kiss me . . . breathe your warm breath into my body. . . ."

He kissed her fiercely, hungrily, rocking her limp body as a mother rocks an injured child. Her face turned ashen; her long lashes lay like dark smudges on her waxen cheeks.

"Cold . . . so cold," she breathed. "Keep . . . me . . . warm. . . ."

Her lips sought his again. Then her hand fell limp on the burgeoning grass.

Conan held her close until Subotai touched his shoulder and silently shook his head. Then he buried his face in her hair.

While the sun still climbed the azure sky, three horsemen reined their lathered beasts beside the shaman's door. Conan dismounted with the limp form of Valeria in his arms, as Subotai flung himself from the lead mount and hurried to release the thongs that bound the princess to the saddle of her horse.

The ancient witch-man hurried forward to meet them. He peered down at Conan's fragile burden and touched one dangling wrist. The eyes he raised in answer to Conan's silent question were sympathetic and devoid of hope. Valeria was dead.

The Cimmerian bore the girl's slight body into the shaman's hut. Subotai, pointing to the captive princess, called after him, "I'll stay outside and guard this baggage. You'll want to be alone a while."

With the help of the old hermit, Conan laid Valeria on a blanket and stripped off her soiled and sodden clothing, in order to sponge away the blood and blackened pigment from her pale flesh. The great jewel stolen from the Tower of the Serpent still spilled its frozen fire across the torn breast of the warrior woman.

Glowering, Conan removed the Serpent's Eye, slung it about his own neck, and tucked it into his tunic.

"That gem," said the wizard, "how came the woman by it?"

"It's just a bauble that I gave her," growled the Cimmerian. "I have no wish to talk about it."

The shaman shrugged and continued to prepare Valeria for immolation. Together they dressed her in a fine silk shift that she had bought in Shadizar to wear on holidays. They crossed her hands upon her breast, and within them placed her sword. They rubbed sweet-smelling herbs upon her brow and combed her long hair.

"She's beautiful," quavered the shaman. "Like a bride."

"Would that she were!" muttered Conan, hastily leaving the hut to help Subotai to gather firewood along the shores of the Vilayet Sea.

The sun was a fiery ball low in the west when the last piece of driftwood was laid on the funeral pyre. Atop the

largest mound it stood, amid the burial places of ancient
warriors and kings; and the slabs that marked their resting
places formed a guard of honor all around it. Thither Conan
carried Valeria and gently laid her down. There in the rosy
sunset, she looked very young, a child asleep.

Subotai helped the old wizard up the slope with a
lighted taper in his trembling hands. Conan regarded his
love with brooding eyes and slowly chanted a mournful
Pit-fighter's song:

> Blood and vengeance
> My sword is singing
> Through bone and flesh.
> The way of the warrior
> Is ever death.

Having bid Valeria a last adieu, the Cimmerian
reached for the flaming torch and, stepping forward,
touched the flame to the dry wood. The fire licked up
around her alabaster beauty, burning with an incandescent
brilliance. A breeze, sighing from the sea, lifted her hair in
gentle fingers and was gone. Unwavering, the smoke rose
into the darkening sky, as if reaching for the evening star.

Conan stood like a figure carved in stone. Subotai
sobbed softly, tears running down his cheeks. The wizard,
roused from mumbling incantations, stared at him.

"Why weep you so, Hyrkanian? Was she so much to
you?" he asked.

Subotai wiped away a tear and cleared his throat.

"She was a friend to me, but she was everything to
him," the small man said. "But he is a Cimmerian and must
not weep. So I do weep for him."

The shaman nodded as he pondered the diverse ways
of men from foreign lands.

The fire burned to coals and then to ash, and the night
wind scattered the ashes far and wide. Through it all, Conan
stood motionless. Then, when the last ash vanished, he
turned to Subotai and the shaman, saying, "Now we must
get ready."

"Ready for what?" asked Subotai.

"For them to come against us."

XVI

The Battle

There was little sleep in the shaman's hut that night. The old wizard huddled in his shabby cloak and watched the young giant whose life had been so dearly bought. Conan sketched battle plans with charcoal on the well-scrubbed hearth. Subotai kept an eye on Yasimina, who lay in the old man's bed, tied to a bedpost.

When dawn burnished the still waters of the Vilayct Sea, the small house became a beehive of activity. Pallets were rolled up and the stewpot set to warming on its hook above a fresh-lit fire. Subotai slipped out to forage for supplies of war. The old man puttered among his piled effects for remnants of arms and armor or for things that might be so employed.

Yasimina sat on the side of the bed, staring at the Cimmerian. Her eyes sparkled with anger; her rose-petal mouth was inverted by a sneer.

"Enjoy this day, barbarian dog," she spat, "for it will be your last."

Conan looked around at her and raised his heavy brows.

"My serpent king knows where you are," she continued. "He has seen your fire and will come, as surely as the sun has risen in the east. And he will slay you."

"Are you a prophetess, then?" growled Conan. "I think not—just a foolish girl. I know not why your father loves you so."

He walked over to the irate princess, seized her chin in his large hand, and glared down into her fiery eyes. Softly, he said: "I was born on a battlefield. . . . The first sound I heard was a scream. . . . The prospect of a battle does not frighten me."

"It frightens me no more!" Yasimina flung back at him. "For my lord will lead his minions to my rescue. My lord . . . and future husband, Thulsa Doom."

Conan smiled grimly. "Then you shall see the battle, blow by blow. And be right there to greet him when he comes for you."

The girl paled slightly as the barbarian untied her from the bedpost and flung her, sacklike, over his shoulder. Striding up the side of the nearest mound, he tethered her against a stele.

"Here you can see it all. And he who comes for you can find you readily."

Subotai called from below, and Conan descended the slope to find the Hyrkanian cradling an armful of bamboo poles. These he dropped with a clatter.

"They'll do for stakes," he said, picking one up and slicing an end at an angle to make a crude spear.

"Where did you find them?" asked Conan, beginning to whittle points on the ends of other poles.

"Down by the sea—behind the tall grasses." Presently, when the last sharpened stake lay on the pile, Subotai said: "Doom's likely to come directly from the mountain. Should we not dig the trench on the far side of the mound?"

"Aye," said the Cimmerian, "and we'll cover it with thin poles strewn with sod."

"If we have time," said Subotai dourly. "I'll fetch shovels from the wizard's root cellar."

Soon the two men were hard at work. All morning the earth flew, and the trench took shape. Although the small thief had to rest from time to time, Conan continued like a tireless machine. His mighty muscles, fueled by implacable hatred and lust for revenge, endowed him with a reserve of power beyond imagining, and he excavated thrice as much as an ordinary man.

The trench was dug and the sharpened poles well-seated when the wizard brought them bread and cheese and a draft of home-brewed beer.

"Do you plan to make your stand here?" he asked.

"Here, or up on yonder mound," said Conan.

The oldster's glance followed Conan's pointing finger. He nodded. "Many battles were fought here in the ancient time," he said. "At night the shades of the slain chant grisly tales of combat."

"Today there'll be a battle like no other—two against many. Old man, if we fall, perhaps you'll sing a song of us when we are gone," said Conan.

"Or to us, if we stay a while," added Subotai cheerfully.

"I'll take some food and drink to Osric's spitfire," said Conan. "We can't have her a ghost if we hope to claim a ransom."

Climbing the mound, the barbarian offered Yasimina some of the wizard's humble food. She made a face at the rude fare and glared at the giver, but Conan noted with amusement that she ate and drank with eager speed.

Still, she was not mollified. After finishing her meal, she taunted him. "It won't be long now."

Conan answered, "No, not long."

Rejoining Subotai, who was busy fashioning arrows to replenish his supply, Conan set about cleaning and sharpening their swords. As he burnished the great Atlantean blade, he thought of his boyhood, of the power of his arch-enemy, of the skills and cunning that a fighting man must have to overcome weight of numbers and brute force.

He noted with satisfaction that Subotai had been a great help, for the canny Hyrkanian was wise about ploys and stratagems. His nomadic people, though a warrior race, were often outnumbered in their feuds and dependent on trickery to worst their enemies; and his knowledge of such matters would prove valuable in the coming contest.

Thus willingly Conan worked with Subotai to strengthen their defenses. They set light poles across the trench, and covered them with a thin layer of turf to look like solid ground. They studied the slabs high on the burial mound, and chose those which offered most protection. They set a quiver of arrows, a supply of throwing stones, and a skin of drinking water in their makeshift fort. Yet, surveying these preparations, they found them inadequate.

"The hidden trench should take care of five horses and their riders," said Subotai, wiping his sweating brow.

"There'll be many more than that," growled Conan.

"Perhaps these warrior ghosts will lend a hand," said Subotai with a mirthless grin. "Two men can do so much, no more."

"You are dead men walking, for all your preparations," said Yasimina, with a defiant toss of her sable locks. "When my lord and his people come . . ."

Yasimina stopped in mid-sentence. The men glanced at each other and reached for their swords. Below them on the hill came the sound of metal scraping metal—a clangor unlike any they had ever heard before. They whirled, sinews tensed for action. Then from Conan's lungs burst a gargantuan laugh.

Coming toward them slowly was the old shaman clothed in ancient armor from head to knee; in his arms he bore an array of breastplates, helmets, and spears. Subotai raced towards him, shouting excitedly, "Where did you get this stuff, old man?"

"From the dead." The wizard grinned. "A gift from the dead. You will find more below." He nodded his head in the direction of his hut.

As Subotai ran down the mound to gather up greaves, swords, axes, arrows, and a bundle of javelins, Conan picked out a fine breastplate and examined it.

"From the dead, you say? But this is strong iron, freshly refurbished. How came it from a grave?"

"You have forgot that I have skill in magic. If I could rekindle your flickering spark of life, it is a lesser feat to beg a gift from those who sleep beneath this mound. Besides, the gods are pleased with you. They will watch the coming battle."

"And will they help?" asked the Cimmerian.

"No, that they cannot do."

"They may not like the show they're watching," growled Conan. "We're only two against . . ."

The wizard interrupted. "We are three."

"Are you joining us, then, in the fight?" demanded Conan in surprise.

"Why not? Why not?" rejoined the oldster. "If you fall, they will slay me, too, for harboring you. So I must aid you all I can." With a fleeting smile, he added, "I still know a trick or two."

As the shaman wandered off to inspect the defenses, the Cimmerian donned a hauberk of fine mesh mail, a steel helmet, and greaves of thin bronze. He placed a sturdy shield and an axe at his chosen stand, and thrust a row of javelins point first into the loose soil, so that they would be ready when needed.

Meanwhile, Subotai had returned, well-armed and brimming with exuberance. Surrounded by his favorite weapons—his sword, his great bow, and plenty of arrows—in addition to his new-found arsenal of knives, and swords, and spears, his indomitable confidence bubbled like a spring of clear water that refreshed his dour companion.

"I wonder why they are so long in coming!" said Subotai. "Are they afraid of us, or have they forgotten us already?"

Yasimina regarded the Hyrkanian as if he were a noxious insect. "Fool, do you not know this is a holy day, set apart by Set for prayers and relaxation? None may bestir himself until the sun goes down."

"Why didn't you say so sooner?" rumbled Conan. "You might have had some supper."

"I would not make things easier for you, barbarian, no matter what I have to do without. You are the enemy of Set."

The sun hung on the horizon, and purple shadows stole across the plain that stretched between the burial mounds of ancient kings and the brooding Mountain of Power, the heart of Doom's invisible empire. From their places of concealment, Conan, Subotai, and the wizard stared out at the darkening wasteland and waited. The waiting gnawed at

their nerves, for they knew that, once darkness swept up the
embers of the dying day, the beast-men would attack.

"What is that sound?" asked Subotai, startled, as an
eerie chanting wafted across the mound. Peering cautiously
from their hiding places, they saw the princess standing in
her bonds, with the wind in her long hair. She was looking
out across the barren land toward the mountain and the
setting sun. The last rays kissed her upturned face and tinted
her naked arms and shoulders a ruddy gold.

The song she sang was strangely melodic; and as its
volume rose, its pensive yearning changed to a passionate
seduction, which nearly overwhelmed her listeners. Despite
her soiled and ragged garments, she looked every inch a
priestess and a leader of men.

"What now?" mused the shaman, as he regarded the
sensuous writhing of the girl and perceived the seductive
magic in her chant.

Subotai, like one entranced, listened to the unearthly
melody and murmured, "How beautiful! What is it that she
sings?"

"Pay no heed!" said Conan. "It is some snake god's
hymn, designed to lure the innocent to Set and to destruction. Heed it not!"

As the stars filled the dark vault of heaven, Conan in
his lonely vigil looked up into the windswept sky. Seldom
had he prayed to Crom, god of the Cimmerians, for he had
learned that the immortal gods have little interest in the
affairs of men. Still, facing almost certain death, the
barbarian breathed a supplication.

"Crom, I have no tongue for prayer, and to you the
outcome of this battle does not matter. Neither you, nor any
other, will remember why we fought or how we died.

"But valor pleases you, Lord Crom, and to me it is
important. This night three brave men stand against many
—that you may remember.

"And for my courage and my blood, I ask one thing
alone: grant me revenge before I die."

The princess ceased her chanting, and stillness lay
upon the darkling land. A wind moaned faintly through the
long grasses. A flock of waterfowl, uttering their plaintive

cries, passed overhead and vanished into darkness. Somewhere a cricket chirped.

Lulled by the quiet, and depleted from the Herculean labors of the day, Conan rested, leaning on the handle of his axe. Suddenly, he knew not why, he raised his head and stared into the deepening shadows. His barbarian instincts told him that something was about to happen.

Like figures materializing out of Conan's boyhood nightmares, a score of mounted riders, black against the gray and shrouded passage of the day, exploded into a storm of trampling hooves and clanking armor. They thundered toward the mound on which Conan and Subotai had set up their defenses; above the standard-bearer's head floated the well-remembered banner of two writhing serpents with fanged mouths, intent upon upholding the black orb of a ragged sun.

Faceless in their ornate helms, the minions of the snake god raised their spears and swords and howled like wolves beneath a gibbous moon. Before they reached the mound, the earth seemed to open up beneath the hooves of the foremost riders, and three horsemen and their mounts pitched into the spear-impaling pit prepared by the Cimmerian and his companion.

Another horse struggled out of the cruel trap and, unmindful of its disabled rider, galloped off across the plain. The beast-man climbed out after it and limped away in futile pursuit of his errant mount.

Other horses, spurred by expert riders, overleaped the hidden barricade or rode around it, and pounded up the slope to search out the enemy. The barbarian stepped from the protection of a stele and stood, a grim giant in the fading light, for all to see. As one rider thundered down upon him, he hurled a javelin and heard a thud as it struck. A moment later, another rider was upon him. Conan hurled his axe and saw it sink into an armored chest.

A second javelin speared a horse. The animal bucked and threw its rider; then, galloping a short distance, it collapsed and sank to the ground. The beast-man, disregarding his own safety, rushed at the Cimmerian, bellowing a war cry. He threw his hairy torso upon his adversary, unsheathed sword in hand, and brought Conan to his knees. At that moment, a bowstring snapped; and Conan heard the whistle of an arrow. His attacker threw his hands before his face too late. The shaft pierced his eye and drove him screaming from the mound.

Riding with the fury of a storm, another of Doom's men hurtled toward the Cimmerian, lance at the ready. The point made contact with Conan's shield and spun him round. But, even as he turned, the wily barbarian snatched his Atlantean blade from its scabbard, and slashed the beast's belly. Neighing and rolling its eyes, the terrified animal rose on its hind legs and pawed at the stars, as its rider fell stunned at the barbarian's feet. One more stroke of the Atlantean sword sundered the head from the supine body.

Another rider, sighting the Hyrkanian crouched behind a grave marker, galloped up the mound. As he neared Subotai's fragile barricade, the small man straightened up and let fly an arrow. With blood fountaining from his torn body, the beast-man collapsed and rolled from his mount, while the riderless animal cantered away. Uttering a ringing cry of victory, Subotai fitted another arrow into the bowstring.

Two other horsemen, heading up the hillock, wheeled to charge down the mound again. One reached the level ground; the other was impaled on Subotai's arrow point. He rose in his saddle, shrieking in agony; then, with a booted foot caught in his stirrup, he was dragged along the rough ground by his frantic steed.

Below Conan and Subotai, who held to the high ground, moved the wizard, his polished armor shining faintly in the twilight. Thinking the old man mad, Conan sought to give him an avenue of escape, meager though it might be. As three of the enemy rode toward the wizard, brandishing their weapons, the shaman's spear arced out of the darkness and buried its head in the chest of the foremost horseman. The man fell backward, across his horse's rump; and the tightening of the reins brought the animal up so short that it reared, danced on its hind hooves for a moment, and fell backward, pinning the injured rider to the ground.

The guard's companions hesitated for an instant to

regard their fallen comrade; then, beneath their helmets, the color drained from their apelike faces. For even as they watched, the shaft of the pinioning spear began to rock back and forth, as if an invisible hand were trying to pluck it from the dying body. A moment later, it pulled free and flew, butt first, into the outstretched palm of the ancient shaman. The wide-eyed companions wheeled and fled.

Conan's astonishment was short-lived, for another beast-man—this one on foot—moved in on him. The Cimmerian raised his father's sword and dealt his adversary a terrific two-handed blow. The creature parried with the point of a lance, which glanced off Conan's helmet. Swinging the great sword again, he cut the haft of the lance in two; and the beast-man staggered, fell, and rolled howling down the hillside.

Then, in answer to a command, the beast-men drew off to re-form their lines on the level ground. Conan glanced up to see Subotai nocking another arrow. One rider alone remained atop the hillock; he was heading for the stele to which the princess's wrists were bound. As he approached, the girl, who had been crouching in abject terror in the long grass beside the monument during the forays of the beast-men and the spirited defense by the kidnappers, rose with a broad smile on her lips and said: "Rexor, you have come for me! Just sever my bonds and take me to him whom I love."

Rexor paced his warhorse toward the eager girl, who held her wrists up to receive the blow that would set her free. But Rexor's eyes were stern, his mien forbidding, as he raised the axe, which shone with silvered light beneath the rising moon.

Suddenly the princess realized that the axe was aimed, not at her ropes, but at her slender neck. Instinctively, she fell to her knees, and the axe struck sparks as it cut a gash in the ancient gravestone. The grim rider withdrew with a curse, as Subotai's arrow clanged with harmless resonance against his helm.

For a brief moment, the embattled three enjoyed a respite. Subotai approached Conan with an ancient sword in his hand and said, "I've used my last arrow."

The wizard clambered up the slope, clutching the spear

that had struck its target and returned to the hand whence it was thrown.

"Said I not that I still had a trick or two?" he cackled.

"Get ready!" cried Subotai suddenly. "Here they come again!" The remaining guards had dismounted and now trotted toward the trio in a solid phalanx. Up the slope they came, prepared to search out the small band of defenders should they take refuge once more behind the stones that marked the graves of kings. Then, halfway up the hill, they hesitated.

"Attack!" cried Subotai as, spear in hand, he prepared to leap forward to face the inhuman creatures who approached them.

But Conan restrained his ardor. "Their confusion is more feigned than real. I fear a trap," he muttered. "Keep to the higher ground. We have the advantage of position—"

A moment later, swords clashed in wild confusion. Conan cut one brute down and felt the sting of a wound on his left arm. Subotai speared another beast-man in the throat; but even as he fell, one of his fellows grasped the shaft, wrenched it from the Hyrkanian's hand, and pointed the blood-stained tip at him. The small man leaped back, stumbled over a broken slab, and lost his balance. Before he could rise, the guard thrust at him with his own spear. The weapon pierced the Hyrkanian's calf and went on into the earth. As the guard brought up his heavy sword to deal a final blow, the shaman's javelin sped through the gloom and took the beast-man in the heart.

As before, the point was rocked by invisible forces until, loosened, it flew back to its wielder. On the magic weapon came again, to strike down another brutish guard. A third turned, slack-jawed, and ran toward the level ground; but the false ground gave way beneath him, and he fell screaming into the stake-filled pit.

Afire with battle madness, Conan rushed from the shelter of the gravestones, hoping to surprise the lone rider who now galloped up the mound. The Cimmerian's spear rang on armor that gleamed in the moonlight; but the spear shaft shattered against his foe's fine steel, and the warrior rode him down. Steel-shod hooves battered the fallen Cimmerian; a deft sword stroke sent his father's sword clattering against a monument. Another blow tore off Conan's helmet.

Bleeding profusely, Conan struggled to his knees, too weak to stagger to his feet. The horseman wheeled his charger, rode away for a few paces, then wheeled again to make a final charge against his broken adversary. He pushed back the visor of his helmet to reveal the dark and grinning face of Rexor, his cruel eyes sparkling in anticipation of the mortal blow to come.

The Cimmerian reached for his fallen sword and rose. His eyes were slits of blue balefire as he raised the blade in the Pit-fighter's salute and prepared to sell his life as dearly as he might. Laughing at the injured youth's temerity, the giant lieutenant spurred his animal and charged, his sword arm rising for the killing blow.

In that instant a radiant Valeria, arrayed in shimmering armor, with lustrous blonde hair floating beneath a winged helmet of unearthly metal, appeared beside her helpless lover. Her well-muscled limbs were shining in the moonlight; the tulwar she uplifted flashed with blue lightning. As Rexor raised his weapon to smash it down on the barbarian's head, his arm was stayed by her fiery sword. Rexor recoiled before the shining figure who, with a deft cross stroke, whipped her blinding blade across his unguarded eyes. He clapped one gauntleted hand to his face to shield his eyes from the intolerable light, and sat his steed as one transfixed.

Conan gaped at the shining figure, his nape-hairs bristling with superstitious awe. The bright girl turned a laughing face to him, and in his mind he heard her say, *Cimmerian, do you want to live forever?*

As Conan straightened with renewed determination, it was as if the glittering figure in unearthly metal had never been, save that a fading ghostlike glory glimmered against the sky. And Conan remembered the words uttered by Valeria after the wizard, by his magic, had driven off the clutching hands of death and all his minions. She had whispered: *My love is stronger than death. . . . Were I dead and you in peril, I would return from Hell itself to fight beside you.*

The memory of such love gave a generous measure of

pride to the wounded barbarian. Painfully, he made his way to the dark horse on which the lieutenant of Doom sat, nursing his dazzled eyes. He slipped the giant's foot from the nearest stirrup and forced the huge man from his saddle. As Rexor landed, catlike, on his feet, the Cimmerian slapped the horse's rump, and the frightened animal careened away into the darkness.

Conan rushed on Rexor, striking mercilessly at his armored form. Rexor, his eyes recovered from the brilliance, slashed at his younger enemy. Conan, deflecting the blow, ducked and rejoined the fray, driving the big man back with massive, wheeling strokes. Then, with a single overhand blow of the two-handed sword, the Cimmerian drove his steel into the cultist's neck. Rexor remained upright, a tower of muscle rooted to the ground. Then, suddenly, he toppled forward, his armor clanking, and lay still.

Conan took a deep breath and looked around. Subotai, with his leg bandaged and the wizard beside him, stood on the edge of the mound watching a knot of retreating guards gallop toward the Mountain of Power. Soon the maw of night swallowed them.

The silence that had fallen on the deserted battlefield was broken by the girlish voice of Yasimina. The three looked up to find the lean, esthetic figure of Thulsa Doom outlined against the star-decked sky. Elegant in his reptilian armor, he sat his horse proudly and faced the bedraggled girl who was the princess of Zamora, priestess of Set, and his intended bride.

"Master! I told them you would come for me," she trilled. "Unbind me now that I may come to you."

"That cannot be," was the cult leader's stony reply. "They have defiled you, as they defiled my temple precincts."

"Nay, Lord Doom, not so. I have been faithful to you, my lord, my father. Desert me not!"

"You are no longer fit to be my bride."

"Then, Master, I will be your slave, and gladly. Do not leave me here among the enemies of Set!"

"Fear not, my child." Doom's silk-smooth voice was comforting.

Thulsa Doom spoke no further word, but unwound a writhing viper from his neck and, as before, transformed it into a deadly arrow. Yasimina watched without comprehension, but Subotai saw the snake king's movement and guessed what he was going to do. As Doom nocked the magic arrow, the Hyrkanian limped forward, careless of his wound. Just as the missile came hissing through the air, Subotai interposed his shield between the viper-arrow and its intended victim. The arrow thumped into the wood, turned back into a snake, and fell writhing to the ground. The small thief drew his sword and hacked it into pieces.

Yasimina laid her head on her bound wrists and wept hysterically. Conan stalked slowly toward the cult leader, staring at him through slit eyes, and placed himself between the princess and her tormentor. Doom glanced at the sword clutched in the Cimmerian's brown fist—the blade of fine Atlantean steel forged by a village smith so many years ago. And as he looked into the determined face of the barbarian, the cold hand of fear lay on the heart of Thulsa Doom. Shuddering, he spurred his black steed and, wheeling, rode off after the vanquished remnant of his guard.

"Powerful spirits abide hereabouts," said the ancient wizard, adding, "and today they fought for you."

"I know, old man, I know," mumbled Conan, thinking of the shining figure of Valeria. "And you and Subotai did much to win the day."

Then the young giant turned and cupped the princess's face gently in his large hands. "He would have killed you; you know that. First he sent his servant; then he came himself to do it."

The girl nodded dumbly.

Conan continued: "Now I must kill him; for he is evil. And you must take me to him. Are you willing?"

Again the princess nodded, and the sad smile of a lost child flitted across her tear-stained face as he hacked her bonds apart.

"You will understand . . . someday . . . when you are a queen," he said.

Through the remainder of the night, Conan and the shaman, in turn, kept watch over the princess and the wounded man. At dawn, Conan awoke and, looking up, saw the wizard standing beside him. The old man murmured: "Let me see the talisman you took from the slain warrior woman. I would study it in yonder light." Pointing to a narrow shaft of sunlight that had found its way into the hut, he added, "My knowledge may prove useful to you."

Conan removed the gem from his neck and handed it to the old man. The wizard carried the jewel to the window and watched its radiance suffuse his simple abode. At last he spoke: "This is the Eye of Set, is it not? Know you aught of its magical properties?"

"No," said Conan. "To me it is but a bauble to be sold."

"Amongst us wizards, it has much repute. Whence came you on it?"

"We stole it from the Serpent's Tower in Shadizar," confessed the Cimmerian. "We risked our lives to get it."

"No wonder that the faithful guarded it so well, or that they would destroy you to regain it!" exclaimed the wizard. "One of its many powers, they say, is to command the beast-men whom Doom keeps to do his bidding. Raise it before one and command him, and he cannot but obey."

Conan stared in amazement. "Crom, Why did you not tell me this before? It would have saved some desperate hand-play yesterday."

The shaman spread his hands. "I tried to question you about the jewel before; but you refused to speak of it and hid it in your bosom."

Conan bit his lip. "I own you have the right of it, old man. It must have been a trick of that malicious fate, of whom I've heard the learned speak. Well, I yet have work to do; and it may still prove useful to me." So saying, he slipped the cord over his head and once more buried the jewel beneath his garment.

XVII

The Avenging

In the great temple, the Faithful of Set were gathered to hear the exhortation of their master. Hundreds of candles, nursed by loving hands, threw a dim radiance over the chamber, and reflected the eager faces of the congregation. The commingling of young voices, flutes, and brasses made solemn music that reverberated through the cavernous hall and lent an air of sanctity, vastly pleasing to the worshipers of Set.

All became silent, as Thulsa Doom, resplendent in his reptilian armor, mounted the dais and faced his followers. His eyes were dark and filled with sorcery, but there was no humanity in them. He fixed his gaze beyond the uplifted faces massed before him, as if he saw some vision of the future that he alone could see, and intoned: "The day of doom is here. The purging is at last at hand. All who stand against us in high places, all who have lied to you and tried to turn you from me—parents, teachers, judges—all shall depart in a night of blood and fire. Then shall the earth be cleansed and ready to receive the god we worship."

"Set!" moaned the listeners in ecstasy.

The soft, smooth voice of Doom continued. "You, my children, are the pure water that will cleanse the world. You shall destroy all who stand against us. In your hands you hold the eternal light that burns in the eyes of Set!"

"Set!" chorused the audience as one.

Doom lit a candle held by a kneeling priest. "This flame," he said, "shall burn away the darkness and light your way to paradise, if you but act when I do call on you."

Not many miles from the citadel of Thulsa Doom, two horses trotted side by side. One bore the slight form of Princess Yasimina, clad in a silken robe from the saddle bags of Valeria. The other, a larger beast, carried a man dressed in the leathern armor and face-encasing helmet of a guard of Thulsa Doom. Above the pounding hoofbeats, had any been there to listen, the following words drifted, like floating petals on a springtime breeze:

"I loved him, and he tried to kill me! Why did he that?"

Conan—for it was he—shrugged. "I do not know. But so long as he lives, you are in danger—and my prayers for vengeance go unanswered. Doom must die."

"I would that Subotai were here to aid you."

"But he lies wounded in the shaman's care," said Conan.

"What help can I be on a mission such as this?" Yasimina's voice held a trace of her former petulance.

"You must lead me to the Master, as you call him. None knows the ways of the hollow mountain so well as one who has lived there."

The girl stared at the mountain that had been her home. Then she shivered.

"I still worship him. How can I help with his destruction?"

"You must do it. For yourself and for Zamora."

"For my country? How so?"

Gently Conan answered her: "You have seen the sun rise. It drives away the terrors of the dark, and from its light foul things that love the darkness cower and hide. You must be the sunrise of Zamora."

Yasimina nodded; but tears were in her eyes.

Boldly, Yasimina rode to the gates of the mountain citadel; boldly, Conan, in the guise of a guardsman, followed her. The sentries, subhuman beings as they were, knew nothing of the girl's abduction or their master's disavowal of her. The gates swung wide; their mounts were stabled.

Head held high, as befitted a priestess of Set, the princess walked up the broad avenue that led to the snake god's temple. She paused to dabble her fingers in the fragrant pool of the fountain at the foot of the wide stairs, and glanced briefly at the armed man who followed her. Then, with a composure that her beating heart belied, she and her attendant entered the sanctuary.

In the dark recesses of the assembly room, their unnoticed figures moved on silent feet. A fugitive gleam of candlelight failed to betray the features of the princess, impassive and thoughtful. Behind the throng of worshipers, a score of brutish guards stood armed; but they did not mark the passage of the newcomers. Their attention was riveted on the cult leader, who, raising his arms, continued his exhortation:

"Know that, on the hard roads you now go forth to follow, weariness and heartache may be your lot. Hunger and loneliness may walk beside you, and loved ones become your enemies. Yet ever Set will walk before, and all who dare to stand against him shall you kill, until the whole wide world is his."

Conan peered at Yasimina. Strange emotions—sorrow, love, and hate—chased one another across the face of the princess as she looked upon the man who, she thought, had loved her, but who would have spilled her life as casually as one throws away the dregs of a wine cup.

Behind his helmet, Conan's eyes were agleam with calm ferocity. His was no longer a mission of revenge; to rid the earth of evil such as this—this was his destiny. All the days of his life, he thought—all the years of toil and suffering on the Wheel of Pain, all the months of training in the skills and wiles of a Pit fighter, all the weary hours of wandering, homeless, across the uncaring land—were but preparation for this moment.

On the dais, Doom stood tall and silent, holding aloft a lighted candle. His face was upturned as if to drink in the radiance of the flame. At his feet, one of the lesser priests resumed the ritual. To his hypnotic chant, the bodies of the worshipers swayed in rhythm, like half-coiled serpents weaving before a snake charmer.

"Blind your eyes, mystic serpent," intoned the priest. *"Kabil sabul; Kabil Kabil; Kabil hakim*! Lift blind eyes to the moon. Whom call ye forth from the gulfs of night? What shadow falleth between the light and thee? Look into the eyes of such a one, O Father Set. Look and blast his soul to shriveled dust! Kill him, kill him, kill him! And all who love him, kill!"

The rapt throng echoed: "Kill!"

With stately tread the chanting priest moved forward, bearing his lighted taper upraised above his head. Thulsa Doom, stranger from the East, sorcerer, high priest of Set, magnificent in his snakelike plates of polished mail, walked like a conqueror behind his acolyte. The faithful, row by row, fell in behind him, each intent on keeping his candle flame from flickering out. At the great portal Doom paused and turned to bestow a final blessing on the cohorts he was about to fling into the world to do his evil bidding.

As he raised a hand in benediction, a wave of consternation broke over the assemblage, as ripples from a falling pebble disturb the surface of a pool. The spell of the devotions broke and faltered into silence. A hundred pairs of eyes sought to pierce the shadows beside the open doors.

As Doom looked around to see the cause of this disturbance, his brutish guards sprang into position between their master and his followers. Linking arms, they formed a living chain through which none could break, should any seek to do so, and awaited further orders.

Conan strode forth into the candlelight with the slow-paced steps of a stalking panther, his father's sword in his right fist. He moved with a strange inevitability, like a tide sweeping in across the sand. The lead priest shrank away, unnerved by the Cimmerian's calm certitude that Fate was guiding him; but Doom faced the barbarian squarely, with neither fear nor wonder in his cold, reptilian eyes.

"Fear him not!" said Doom. "He is but a mortal man. He cannot stem our tide of victory now. Guards! Seize him!"

Before any of the slow-witted beast-men could react to

the command, Conan held up the huge gem that he had stolen from the temple in Shadizar and repeated the words learned from the shaman.

"Back, in the name of Set!" roared the Cimmerian. *"Podozhditye, nazad!* Back and restrain the others!"

At the sight of the crimson Eye of Set, the guards flinched, as from the flesh-tearing sting of a whip. They shrank back, but their line held. The worshipers could only watch in helpless amazement, while the priest fled, screaming, down the broad staircase.

Doom's lean, ascetic face remained devoid of expression; but the keen eyes searching Conan's face seemed to delve into his very soul. In the Cimmerian youth the sorcerer saw strength. There was humanity, too, and this he read as weakness. He smiled a thin, triumphant smile as he caught and held the barbarian's gaze with his strangely snakelike eyes.

"You have come to me at last, Conan, as a son to his father," Doom began in his soft, hypnotic voice. "And rightly so, for who is your father if not I? Who gave you the will to fight for life? Who taught you to endure? I am the wellspring whence flows your strength. If I were gone, your life would have no purpose."

To the young Cimmerian it seemed that the Master's eyes expanded until they swallowed up the universe. He stood in a vast nothingness between the stars, seeing only those glowing, unwinking eyes. The seductive voice droned on.

"Without me, it will be as if you never had existed. My son, I am your friend, and not your enemy!"

For a long moment, the dark eyes of Doom, redolent with unearthly power, held Conan spellbound. Then Conan blinked his ensorcelled eyes and, summoning all the courage that was in him, tore his gaze free. In that instant, the Cimmerian flung up his left arm and suspended the Eye of Set an arm's length from the face of Thulsa Doom. Doom stared fixedly at the swinging jewel, then raised eyes wide with horror to meet Conan's vengeful glare.

Before the frozen faces of the faithful, Doom's neck lengthened. His jaws elongated; his nose shrank and disappeared; his forehead retreated; his lips thinned and vanished. His dark eyes rounded into lidless orbs and a purple tongue flicked out to test the air. Thulsa Doom bore the scaly serpent head of the ancient snake-men—those timeless enemies of all mankind.

As one, the congregation gasped. A shudder rippled through the silent throng. The princess, watching from the shadows, uttered a half-choked cry as tears of pity, mixed with horror and relief, coursed down her cheeks.

Conan's sword sighed as it swept up in a great arc and clove the swaying snake head from the human body. The body fell backward and lay, writhing, like a trampled serpent, at the top of the wide steps. The severed head rolled slowly down the long flight of stairs and came to rest beside the fountain pool.

Conan watched the gory object fall into the purple shadows of the dying day. Then, half to himself, he spoke: "My father was the light of day; Thulsa Doom, my night. Yet in one thing he spoke true. What matters is not the steel within the blade, but the steel within the man."

Rousing himself, Conan turned to face the guards who, obedient to his last command, still held the assemblage at bay. Raising the Eye of Set once more, he said: "You who were guards of Doom, go back to the caves from which he called you. . . . And find another source of meat. Go."

As the beast-men melted away, Conan looked at the former followers of Thulsa Doom. Some stared dejectedly about them, as if they knew not where they were, nor how they came to be in this strange place. Some sobbed for their dead leader. Others wept for their lost Paradise, and their moans undulated like the restless singing of the surf.

Conan masked his pity with rough words: "I know you feel like orphans, but you all have homes to go to, and a welcome waiting there. I have none. Yet I'm content, and you should be so, too; for this night we are free. Go and get ready for the journey."

The barbarian stood at the threshold of the temple, as Doom's children straggled down the long staircase. One by one, they tossed their lighted candles into the pool, to flicker for a moment before hissing into nothingness.

After the last departed, Conan wiped clean the sword that had so long consumed his thoughts and dreams. Seating himself beneath the portal, he watched the little flames wink out. With his father's sword across his knees, he remembered the past and wondered what the future years might bring. Yasimina, who with the others had extinguished her candle—the symbol of Doom's intended conquest of the world—remounted the deserted stairs. She crouched on the step beside Conan, seeking his strength, and yet too humbled to risk disturbing his reverie. So they passed the weary night.

As pale dawn heralded the break of a new day, Conan perceived a strange change in the scene before him. The stone steps had become pitted and eroded, as by ages of exposure to the elements. The garden shrubs and flowers all were wilted, and the pavement around the half-drained pool was marked by muddy footprints. The ceremonial roadway beyond lay cracked and flaking, as if some spell, dredged from the womb of time to hold it firm, were broken. Behind him, the façade of the cavern temple was crumbling; and, as he watched, bits of stone fell with a clatter to the doorsill.

The tension had drained out of him; he felt at peace. But mingling with his sense of destiny fulfilled was an eagerness to be gone from this foul place—to put the scene and all its memories behind him. Conan rose. The princess scrambled to her feet.

"What now?" she asked.

"Subotai and I will take you home," he answered gruffly. "Your father will be glad to see you."

"My father is dead," said Yasimina. "A messenger from Shadizar arrived but five days past to say that he'd been slain by Yaro's minions."

"Then you are queen and will be needed in Zamora to rule your troubled land."

"But what of Yaro? He will not accept me on the throne."

"I'll deal with Yaro, never fear. Now it is time to go."

"But," the girl persisted, "there are other Towers of Set, and other leaders throughout Zamora. What of them?"

Conan stood silent, thinking. At last he said: "Many

will be broken and deserted, because their purpose died
with Thulsa Doom. The cult may long continue here and
there, for snakes are hard to kill. The worship of Set may
even wax again; but not, I think, within our lifetime."

Yasimina raised her anxious eyes to the barbarian's
face and smiled.

As summer donned the russet dress of autumn, Conan,
brave in new garments and bright mail, with a scarlet cloak
floating from his shoulders, galloped a black stallion beside
Zamora's fileds of ripening grain. At length he caught up
with the man he followed—a small Hyrkanian riding a
shaggy steppe pony. After a brief greeting, they dismounted.

"Why did you ride off without a word?" asked Conan.

Subotai shrugged. "They told me that the Queen had
offered you a place beside her on the throne." The small
man grinned and added, "I thought you'd be too busy with
your . . . er . . . royal duties to have time for an old
comrade-in-arms. Why are you here? I took no more than
my fair share of the Queen's reward for the Serpent's Eye
—though why she wanted it I can't imagine."

Conan looked faintly embarrassed. "As I did, before I
left the city."

"You mean you turned the lady's offer down?"

Conan grunted. "When I wear a crown, it will be won
by my own sword, not given as a dowry."

Subotai sighed. "Strange are the ways of Cimmerians!
How did you dispose of Yaro? Would that I had been beside
you then, instead of doing guard duty at the palace!"

Conan shrugged. "The fighting came to little. When
the folk of Shadizar heard that Doom was dead, the black
priest's followers turned on him. Before I had a chance to
sword him, his own people tore him limb from limb."

"Whither go you now?" asked Subotai.

"South and west. I'm heading for the sea," said Conan.
"And what of you?"

The Hyrkanian pointed. "North and east, to my homeland. Shall we ever meet again?"

Conan grinned. "The world is not wide enough to keep

such rogues as we apart for long. We shall meet again, but Crom knows where and when."

"If only at the gates of Hell," laughed Subotai.

"Until that day, good fighting!"

The two friends embraced, slapping each other's shoulders. Then they swung into the saddle.

"What's in the south and west that draws you thither?" called Subotai.

"Gold, jewels, beautiful women, and fine red wine!" roared Conan.

Then, with a wave of farewell, they rode away, each toward a different horizon.

The fabulous adventures of

CONAN

Movie viewers all across the country are being thrilled by the film exploits of the mighty Conan in CONAN THE BARBARIAN. But the sensational action doesn't stop there. You can follow the steel-muscled giant in these six riveting adventures.

CONAN THE SWORDSMAN by *L. Sprague de Camp, Lin Carter and Bjorn Nyebrg*
Conan engages demons and evil sorcerers while living by his code: spare no coward, and let the strong survive!

CONAN THE LIBERATOR by *L. Sprague de Camp, and Lin Carter*
In the proudest kingdom of the great Hyborian world, brave men cowered, for a madman wore the crown. Now Conan, sword in hand, girds himself for a terrible confrontation.

CONAN: THE SWORD OF SKELOS by *Andrew Offutt*
Not even the barbarious strength of Conan is as great as the murderous tyrant Akter Khan and the deadly sorcery of the most terrible talisman of all.

CONAN: THE ROAD OF KINGS by *Karl Edward Wagner*
Plucked from the gallows by the daring rebels of White Hose, Conan joins his rescuers in their blood-soaked struggle to rid Zingara of its hated despot.

CONAN AND THE SPIDER GOD by *L. Sprague de Camp*
With a price on his head, Conan must pursue kidnappers into the temple of the monstrous spider god whose opal eyes burn like malevolent suns.

CONAN THE REBEL by *Poul Anderson*
Conan storms into the dreaded land of Stygia to free the slaves of the evil sorcerer of Khemi.

Read all of these thrilling CONAN books, available wherever Bantam paperbacks are sold.